No ... ...ving my baby?

Trudy—hopeless romantic, office gossip, can't keep a secret. *If it's not her, she might know who it is!*

Lauren Connor—dates a lot, trying out new looks to impress her boss, was out sick with stomach flu. *hmm...*

Sharon Davies—recently trapped in an elevator with a major client, blushes whenever he's around, looking a little green lately. *Could she be carrying my baby?*

Leila—makes eyes at me. *Is it more than a crush?*

Maggie Steward—my personal assistant, married? wants children, clock is ticking. *She would never go to a sperm bank!*

Julia Parker—worries that her endometriosis could make her infertile. No man in her life. *Definite sperm bank material!*

Jennifer Martin—eight months pregnant. Is it her late fiancé's baby? *Is it mine?*

KANE HALEY, INC.
Chicago, IL

Dear Reader,

We've been trying to capture what Silhouette Romance means to our readers, our authors and ourselves. In canvassing some authors, I've heard wonderful words about the characteristics of a Silhouette Romance novel—innate tenderness, lively, thoughtful, fun, emotional, hopeful, satisfying, warm, sparkling, genuine and affirming.

It pleases me immensely that our writers are proud of their line and their readers! And I hope you're equally delighted with their offerings. Be sure to drop a line or visit our Web site and let us know what we're doing right—and any particular favorite topics you want to revisit.

This month we have another fantastic lineup filled with variety and strong writing. We have a new continuity—HAVING THE BOSS'S BABY! Judy Christenberry's *When the Lights Went Out...* starts off the series about a powerful executive's discovery that one woman in his office is pregnant with his child. But who could it be? Next month Elizabeth Harbison continues the series with *A Pregnant Proposal.*

Other stories for this month include Stella Bagwell's conclusion to our MAITLAND MATERNITY spin-off. Go find *The Missing Maitland.* Raye Morgan's popular office novels continue with *Working Overtime.* And popular Intimate Moments author Beverly Bird delights us with an amusing tale about *Ten Ways To Win Her Man.*

Two more emotional titles round out the month. With her writing partner, Debrah Morris wrote nearly fifteen titles for Silhouette Books as Pepper Adams. Now she's on her own with *A Girl, a Guy and a Lullaby.* And Martha Shields's dramatic stories always move me. Her *Born To Be a Dad* opens with an unusual, powerful twist and continues to a highly satisfying ending!

Enjoy these stories, and keep in touch.

Mary-Theresa Hussey

Mary-Theresa Hussey,
Senior Editor

Please address questions and book requests to:
Silhouette Reader Service
U.S.: 3010 Walden Ave., P.O. Box 1325, Buffalo, NY 14269
Canadian: P.O. Box 609, Fort Erie, Ont. L2A 5X3

Judy Christenberry

WHEN THE LIGHTS WENT OUT...

SILHOUETTE *Romance*®

Published by Silhouette Books

America's Publisher of Contemporary Romance

Special thanks and acknowledgment are given to Judy Christenberry for her contribution to the HAVING THE BOSS'S BABY series.

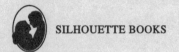 SILHOUETTE BOOKS

ISBN 0-373-19547-8

WHEN THE LIGHTS WENT OUT...

Visit Silhouette at www.eHarlequin.com

Printed in U.S.A.

Books by Judy Christenberry

Silhouette Romance

The Nine-Month Bride #1324
Marry Me, Kate #1344
Baby in Her Arms #1350
A Ring for Cinderella #1356
†*Never Let You Go* #1453
†*The Borrowed Groom* #1457
†*Cherish the Boss* #1463
†*Snowbound Sweetheart* #1476
Newborn Daddy #1511
When the Lights Went Out… #1547

*The Lucky Charm Sisters
†The Circle K Sisters

JUDY CHRISTENBERRY

has been writing romances for fifteen years because she loves happy endings as much as her readers do. She's a bestselling author for Harlequin American Romance, but she has a long love of traditional romances and is delighted to tell a story that brings those elements to the reader. A former high school French teacher, Judy devotes her time to writing. She hopes readers have as much fun reading her stories as she does writing them. She spends her spare time reading, watching her favorite sports teams and keeping track of her two adult daughters.

"You're not nervous, are you?"
Andy asked.

"Not yet, Andy. I feel well prepared for this job. Besides, if I find a problem, I can always bring it to you, can't I? You're not going to refuse to speak to me, are you?"

He chuckled. "You know I won't. And Mr. Waterton is a good man to work for."

An uproar of laughter interrupted them, and they both looked at the closed door. Sharon automatically smiled, but a frown replaced it as something in the two voices, fainter now but still audible, made her pause.

"What did you say Mr. Waterton's name was?" she asked.

"It's John," Andy answered.

"Oh, yes, right," she agreed, still worried.

"But he usually asks everyone to call him—"

The door opened. "There you are," Kane called out. "Andrew Huffman, Sharon Davies, I'd like you to meet Jack Waterton."

Jack. The Jack of her dreams. The father-of-her-baby Jack. Thank goodness she was already sitting down.

Prologue

Kane Haley leaned back in his chair, thinking about his luncheon appointment. He just had to take care of this one little chore and then he'd—

A voice on the phone interrupted his thoughts. He'd been put on hold several minutes ago, and he'd been getting a little impatient.

"Uh, I'm sorry, Mr. Haley."

"I don't understand. You're sorry about what?"

"The—the sperm donation you made was accidently dispersed." The man had rushed through that sentence.

Kane's chair snapped into an upright position as he took in the meaning. Slowly, he said, "By dispersed, you mean some woman took—some woman is having my baby?" His voice grew louder. "Some—who?"

"We can't tell you that, but it only happened because the woman was an employee of your company, and that's why the clerk thought your sperm was what she wanted. And—and we're sorry for any inconvenience."

"Any inconvenience? Any—damn it! Give me the woman's name."

"We can't do that, Mr. Haley. We'd be sued."

Kane didn't care if they were sued. Hell, he might sue them himself. He'd given the sperm because his best friend, Bill Jeffers, had discovered he had cancer. He was to begin radiation treatment and wanted to save his own sperm for the future. Kane had gone with him in support, and the counselor they'd visited with had suggested Kane donate sperm also to be held in case his friend's sperm shouldn't work.

He'd just learned his friend's wife was pregnant— the natural way—and he'd decided to ask the sperm bank to destroy his own donation.

Too late.

"When did this happen? Surely you can tell me that?"

"It—it was recent, but I can't give you any more information than that. Thank you."

Then he was listening to a dial tone. He slammed down the receiver. What now? What was he going to do? Should he ask Maggie to—no, he didn't want to explain this problem to her. Maggie was his incredibly efficient assistant who was as strict with him as she was with herself. He couldn't see himself confessing to Maggie that he'd been careless with his sperm!

Okay, so he'd have to handle this himself. He'd—

he'd look at the women among his employees and find out who was pregnant.

And ask them who the father was?

He couldn't ask a question like that. No, he had to have a reason.

After a knock on his door, Maggie entered. "Are you going to lunch?"

"Yes, uh, yes, but I—" Suddenly inspiration struck. "I have a question for you. Do we have any women employees who are pregnant?"

She stared at him, then nodded and said, "Yes."

"I see. Do—do we offer any benefits to them?"

She blinked, her cheeks turning pink.

"We offer medical benefits."

"Ah. I was wondering if we should do more. Like—like create an on-site child-care center? I was reading an article about the benefits to a company that meets its employees' needs."

"Really?"

"Yes. So—so tomorrow, I'm going to do some questioning of our pregnant employees. I'll need a list of them."

"Very well."

"You can get me a list?" he asked, always amazed at Maggie's efficiency.

"I'll do my best."

She laid some papers on his desk and turned to leave.

Tomorrow. Tomorrow he'd find out who was having his baby.

Chapter One

Sharon Davies approached the bank of elevators, pretending her life was perfectly sane, calm, happy.

She had a good job with Kane Haley, Inc., a growing accounting firm in Chicago. She loved her work, she had a great family, the sun was shining...and this morning she'd taken a home pregnancy test.

The elevator door opened, and she didn't move. Someone pushed her from behind. "Come on, lady, I got deliveries to make."

"Sorry," she muttered and stepped to one side. "Go ahead. I'll take the next one."

The messenger, along with several other people, entered the elevator. Then he looked at Sharon. "Come on, there's room."

"No! No, I—I can't." She took another step back.

He stared at her as if she were crazy. Maybe she was. Not many sane people could claim to have gotten pregnant in an elevator. That elevator.

The door closed and Sharon stared at her image in the mirrored doors. She didn't look like a loose woman. She was wearing a conservative gray sheer wool suit, a plum silk blouse with all but the top button closed. Her skirt was slim but of moderate length. Her shoes were low heels. She wasn't trying to catch a man's eye.

She hadn't been trying two months ago either. But she'd been late to work after a terrible morning when everything that could go wrong had. She hated elevators, but she certainly hadn't been tempted to use the stairs to walk up sixteen floors. She enjoyed exercise, but she wasn't crazy.

Another elevator opened. Drawing a deep breath, she entered it, crossing her arms over her chest so no one would notice her hands shaking. She leaned against the wall and closed her eyes. Jack's face filled her head, only today it didn't have a calming affect.

Her eyes filled with unshed tears. They popped open and she blinked several times to dry them. She wasn't going to cry.

The door slid open on the top floor, her floor, and she quickly stepped out. Pasting a smile on her lips, she greeted fellow workers as she hurried to her desk. She felt—safer behind her desk. It wasn't as if anyone could *see* that she was pregnant…yet. The first thing she had to do, however, was make a doctor's appointment.

She was the only member of their department at work, so she grabbed the phone and dialed her doctor's office. A couple of minutes later, she hung up the phone. Tomorrow morning at nine. At least that little errand was taken care of.

She stepped to her boss's office. Andrew Huffman was the closest thing to a father-figure she'd had since her own father had walked out on her mother, leaving his five children. Sharon was the oldest.

The struggle that ensued, still ongoing, had reminded her every day that men—at least some men—couldn't be trusted. Now, with her mother's hard work and her own contributions, starting when she'd gotten a part-time job at fourteen, all her siblings were getting a college education.

When she'd started at Kane Haley Inc., fresh out of high school at eighteen, she'd come to Andrew Huffman's department. He'd encouraged her to learn and grow, using the company training as well as her night classes, to take on more and more responsibility.

She'd completed her degree this August and Andy had been as excited as her. Now, she rapped on his door, knowing he'd be at his desk. He was nearing retirement age and worked from a wheelchair, but he had the energy of men half his age.

"Come in."

"Andy? I have a doctor's appointment for tomorrow morning, so I won't be in until ten or ten-thirty. Is that okay?"

"Sure. Is everything okay?"

"Yes. Just something I need to take care of." She certainly wasn't going to tell anyone about it until she had her pregnancy confirmed by a doctor. She wasn't sure if the home tests were really reliable. Or maybe she was just hoping.

"Okay. I may have some good news for you next week. Your very own project," he exclaimed with a boyish grin.

She tried to look excited. "Really? Any details?"

"Can't tell you yet. But keep up the good work."

She retreated to her desk. She and Andy had talked about her heading up her first project. Without her degree, he couldn't let her take that responsibility, but he'd promised she'd get the chance now.

Yesterday, she would've been thrilled.

Now she wasn't sure she could handle it.

The temptation to call Jen was hard to resist. One of her friends, Jennifer Martin, was the Health Benefits Manager. It was Jen who had inspired her to buy a home pregnancy kit. When Sharon had complained over lunch about fatigue and occasional nausea, Jen had commented that it sounded like pregnancy to her.

Sharon had laughed, along with Jen, because Jen would know. She'd discovered her own pregnancy a month after her fiancé had died in a car wreck.

Jen didn't know she was the inspiration, because she didn't know about the elevator incident. No one did except her and Jack.

If only she knew who Jack was.

"Yes, the test was correct, Miss Davies. You are approximately eight weeks pregnant. Your baby is developing nicely. I foresee no difficulties. I'll write you a prescription for prenatal vitamins and set you up for an examination schedule of every six weeks until you're six months pregnant. It will be every two weeks then, until we're down to the last month. I might change to every week then."

The older woman in the white coat beamed at her as she made notes on the new chart. "Now, who shall I list as the father?"

Sharon stared at her. She'd been coming to Dr. Norman since she'd started working at Kane Haley, Inc., eight years ago. The doctor was on their company plan and was in the same building, convenient.

"Uh, I'm not listing a father's name," she said calmly, folding her hands in her lap.

"You don't know who the father is?" Dr. Norman asked sharply.

"I know who he is, but I don't want his name on the records. It's my baby and I'll provide for it."

"Ah, a married man," the doctor muttered, her lips flattening out as she pressed them tightly together.

Was he? Sharon didn't think so, but she couldn't say for sure. When he'd held her in his arms, caressing her as they talked, sharing the most intimate parts of their lives, he'd told her about his wife and unborn son dying in a car accident. But the accident had been eight years ago.

Maybe he hadn't brought her up to date on his life because—because they were touching each other in an inappropriate way. But she'd been so frightened, so terrified of dying, she had wanted to crawl inside him and hide.

"Miss Davies? Sharon? Are you all right?" the doctor asked.

"Yes, why?"

"You didn't answer my question. I wondered if

your family would— Probably you're okay financially, since you have insurance, but birth is an emotional thing, as well. Will your family help you?''

''Yes, my family will be there for me.''

''I can't help but recommend you notify the father, even if you aren't together anymore. He has the right to know about his impending fatherhood.''

Sharon stared straight ahead. Even if she wanted to tell Jack the results of their strange odyssey, Jack was all she knew. No last name. She wasn't even sure she could identify him. Until the elevator got stuck, she hadn't looked at him. Then, after half an hour, the lights went out.

She knew his scent. A wonderfully male essence that made her think of a fall day and a sexy man, crisp yet tantalizing. She knew his voice, that sexy burr that comforted and excited her and made her forget the danger.

Just not his name.

''I'd like you to take birthing classes. You'll need a partner.'' When Sharon said nothing, she added, ''You can go without a partner, but you'll be more comfortable if you can enlist a friend. Everyone else will be in a couple.''

''Yes. How soon will I start them?''

''Not until you're five months pregnant. Here is some literature for you to study, to get you started. If you have any questions, any at all, call the nurse. Okay?''

The doctor stood, handing her the literature and a prescription.

''Thank you, Doctor.''

Sharon left, hiding the papers in her purse before she ran into someone from her office. She didn't want the information to get out until it had to. Until her body changed so much she couldn't hide it.

The doctor's office was on the twelfth floor. She took the stairway back to her company's floors, fourteen through sixteen. The small cafeteria was on the fifteenth floor and served as the break room also.

She stopped there instead of going straight back to work. Several of her friends waved to her and she hurried over.

"Hi, Sharon, join us," Maggie offered. She was the assistant to Mr. Haley himself, the owner of the company. But she didn't act any differently than Sharon's other friends.

"Let me get some juice before I sit down," Sharon said.

When she returned to the table, Lauren Conner asked, "What happened to your usual diet soda?"

"Oh, I'm fighting a cold and the doctor suggested less soda and more fruit juice."

"Good for you," Maggie said. "I'm getting older and discovering everything you eat affects you. It's gross!"

Both Lauren and Sharon laughed. They were mid-twenties, but Maggie was thirty-three. Still not what most people would consider as over the hill.

"I think you've got a few years, Maggie," Sharon assured her.

"I certainly hope so, but I need all my energy to keep up with Kane."

Jennifer Martin entered the cafeteria and immediately joined them. "Hi. Sorry I'm late. The big boss had some questions for me." She looked at Maggie. "Did you know about this?"

Maggie calmly continued eating a cluster of grapes. "You mean the child-care possibilities?"

"Yes," Jen said.

Sharon immediately sat straighter in her chair.

"On site? Child-care on site?" she asked.

Both Jen and Maggie nodded.

Lauren clapped her hands. "Jen, how wonderful for you! That will help a lot, won't it?"

"It would be wonderful," Jen agreed. "When he asked me about it, I thought I must be dreaming." Jen was more than seven months pregnant and had successfully hidden her pregnancy until recently. "Not that it will be ready right away even if he decides to go ahead with it, but it's something great to look forward to."

"Kane certainly hadn't considered the idea until the last day or so. He said he read an article," Maggie told her. "I gave him a list of pregnant women this morning, but I didn't put anyone on the list who hadn't already announced her pregnancy."

"I didn't let my emotions show, but I almost passed out with surprise," Jen said with a chuckle. "He's decided to form a committee to study the idea. Matt Holder and I are on it. A woman due in a couple of months and a confirmed bachelor! I hope whoever the other members of the committee are, they have some experience with babies!"

"Well, I hope Kane won't be on it. After all, he's

divorced and has no children, so he won't have any experience either,'' Maggie pointed out.

"It's pretty impressive that he thought of the idea, isn't it?'' Sharon said. "He's a very good employer.''

"Yes, he is,'' Maggie agreed, warmth in her voice.

They all suspected Maggie had feelings for her boss, but she'd never admitted to them, and none of them would think of asking her.

Sharon had so much to think about. She finished her juice and stood. "I'd better get to work. I haven't been to the office yet since I had an appointment this morning.''

"How are you feeling? Any better?'' Jen asked.

"Um, yeah. I drank juice instead of a soda. The doctor said I needed more vitamin C. See you!''

She hurried away, afraid she'd blurt out things she needed to keep to herself. But in twenty-four hours, her life had changed so much, it was difficult to take it all in.

"Everything all right?'' Andy asked her as soon as she reported in.

"Yes, fine. Did I miss anything this morning?''

"Nope, just work, and we saved you some,'' he added with a grin.

Sharon smiled back and went to her desk, greeting the other members of the staff as she went. She was so fortunate to work in this department, Special Projects. Everyone was so cheerful.

She knew it all stemmed from Andy. He always had a smile on his face. And who could complain about bills or the sniffles or whatever when their boss was in a wheelchair?

That was what she had decided last night. So she was pregnant. She'd always wanted children, but she didn't have any enthusiasm for marriage. So, now she didn't have to worry about it. Fortunately she lived in an age when women didn't have to force themselves into a marriage they didn't want just because they'd been unfortunate enough—no, not unfortunate. She wasn't going to think that way. There were a lot of women in the world who couldn't get pregnant. She was one of the fortunate ones.

The doctor might recommend telling the father, but *she* didn't. After all, he'd left the hospital without contacting her. They'd been taken in separate ambulances to the nearest hospital after they'd been rescued. When she'd been checked and released, she'd asked about him. The nurse told her he'd already gone.

He obviously had felt he didn't owe her anything, and he didn't want anything to do with her. That much was clear.

She pulled out her work and swept such thoughts away. She had seven months to adjust to being a single parent. She didn't have to devote today to such things.

After lunch, she again had settled down to work when her phone rang.

Andy greeted her and asked if she'd come to his office.

He called her into his office frequently to discuss certain items, calling her his right-hand man. She didn't think anything of it.

When she opened the door however, she discovered

the owner, Kane Haley himself, leaning against a windowsill. Both he and Andy were smiling, so she didn't think there was a problem.

"Good afternoon, Mr. Haley, Andy. Did you need something?"

"Sit down, Sharon," Andy said, gesturing to one of the chairs in front of his desk.

She did so and waited. He looked at Kane and nodded.

"Sharon, you've been working here for almost eight years. Andy raves about you all the time, calling you his right-hand man. I think it's time we made it official."

She stared at him, having difficulty taking his meaning.

"The right-hand part, not the man part," Kane hurriedly added with an even bigger grin. "I can assure you neither one of us objects to your femininity."

She turned to Andy, still not sure what Kane meant.

"He's trying to tell you, my dear, that you now bear the title of Assistant Director of Special Projects, with the appropriate raise, of course."

Sharon felt her jaw drop. That position had been vacated several years ago and Andy had said it was unnecessary.

"Me? I've been promoted? A raise?" Suddenly her mind was filled with all the soon-to-be expenses she'd incur with a child. How perfect! Without even knowing the amount, she was thrilled.

"Oh, thank you, Andy! And Mr. Haley. Thank you so much. I promise I'll work hard."

"You already do, my dear," Andy said with a

smile. "You don't want to overdo it or I'll think you're after my job."

When she began to protest, he shushed her with a few words and a chuckle.

"Well, I'm glad I was here for the announcement, Sharon," Kane said. "It's always encouraging to have happy employees." He shoved away from the window and extended his hand to her.

She stood and shook his hand.

Then, as he turned to go, he came to a halt. "Oh, by the way, Andy, do you have any pregnant women in your department?"

Chapter Two

Sharon abruptly folded into the chair from which she'd risen. "Uh, my knees are shaky from the excitement," she said hurriedly.

"Good," Kane said with a dismissive nod. "I like your enthusiasm." Then he looked at Andy again. "Well?"

"Not that I know of," Andy said, surprised. "Michelle is on maternity leave. She had her baby about six weeks ago. When is she due back, Sharon?"

"Next Monday," Sharon said.

"Yeah, I know about her," Kane said. "But it occurred to me that some women might keep their pregnancies secret for a while, and—and the more women we have who are pregnant, the more the child-care center would benefit us. So I thought—Why wouldn't they tell everyone?"

Sharon blinked and tried to shrink down in her

chair. She didn't want to be a part of this conversation.

"I suppose they're afraid it will affect their careers," Andy said, frowning.

"Would it?" Kane asked. "I don't want my employees punished because of that. What do you think, Sharon?"

"M-me? Uh, no, I don't think women here are punished because they have a—a family."

"Good. So if it's not fear, why would they keep it a secret?"

Sharon knew why she was keeping it a secret. She didn't want to tell anyone about what happened. She was single, which would raise questions. Besides she'd have to reveal her secret soon enough.

Then there was Jen. Her situation was awkward, too, since she wasn't married. With Kane and Andy both staring at her, she said, "Maybe some women don't have husbands, so it's difficult."

"Yeah," Kane agreed, "but what if a woman wanted the pregnancy and, say, went to a sperm bank. Would she hide her pregnancy?"

Sharon thought he looked more intense than ever. What was going on? "I don't know," she muttered.

Kane sighed. "No. I don't either." He looked at Andy. "Let me know if you hear of any new pregnancies, okay?"

"Sure," Andy agreed. He and Sharon remained silent while Kane left the office. Then he looked at Sharon. "That was strange."

"Yes," Sharon said, still tense.

"Here are the papers about your promotion and

how much of a raise you're getting. Look it over and we'll talk later.'' Andy said, smiling again.

Sharon stood and took the papers. "Thank you again, Andy.''

"Nothing to thank me for. You've earned it.''

She moved to the door, still unnerved by everything.

"Oh, by the way, clear your schedule tomorrow. Your project assignment will be ready tomorrow instead of next week. No time to waste.''

She closed the door behind her and took a deep breath. Oh, my. Life seemed to be changing at high speed. She was getting her own project, had received a promotion...and she was pregnant. What else could happen?

She dreamed of Jack that night. It wasn't the first time. After the traumatic experience of believing she was going to die and his saving her mind if not her body, it wasn't surprising.

In fact, she'd welcomed those dreams, just as she focused on Jack every time she entered the elevator now. Those hours spent with him had changed her life in more ways than the pregnancy. She'd been intimate with him because of the comfort and courage he gave her.

She hadn't let a man get close to her in a long time. Once she'd let a man get close, but he'd abandoned her, just as her father had, and had only reinforced her opinion about men.

Even though Jack had walked away when she'd needed him desperately, in the elevator he'd been there for her. So she felt him hold her close in her dreams.

But now, carrying his child, wondering what he would think about that fact, she found the dreams disturbing. She needed to shut Jack out of her mind as well as her life.

When she faced the elevators the next morning, she vowed she wouldn't picture Jack in her mind. She could ride the elevator without his protection. Again she passed up the particular elevator where they'd been trapped. When she entered the next elevator, it was crowded. She tried to stay close to the door, but she ended up in the back because of the crowd.

She concentrated on her breathing, or tried to, but by the time she reached her floor, she was sweating and breathing rapidly. "Out, please," she called desperately, wondering why these people weren't moving when it was the top floor.

By the time she emerged, she felt exhausted and disheveled. She leaned against the wall, taking deep gasps of air.

"Sharon? Are you all right?" Maggie asked.

Sharon whirled around and stared at her friend. "Yes! Of course. It's just that sometimes I think about—I don't like elevators."

"Who could blame you, after being trapped in one. Kane had all of them checked after your experience. I promise it won't happen again," Maggie said with a smile, giving Sharon a little hug. "Why don't you go get a cup of coffee?"

"No, I have—I'm getting my own project to run this morning. I've waited a long time for this day."

"Oh, yes. And it's an important one. John Waterton is an important client. Good for you." With a smile, Maggie moved on and Sharon drew a deep breath. She was okay, she was sure. Of course, now that she knew who the client was, her knees were shaking again. Everyone in the company knew about the Waterton account. Kane Haley had signed them on as a small project about six months ago. It had gone so well, Mr. Waterton had used Kane Haley, Inc., again. Sharon had heard rumors that this next project would be a big one.

Hers. It might be hers.

Excitement took precedence over fear, and she hurried to her desk. If Maggie was right, and she was always right, her project would be very important for the entire company. She would work closely with whoever was in charge to set up a budget, supervise the spending and pay out the funds.

She took another deep breath to calm herself. She wanted to be able to speak coherently, not sound like an idiot.

By the time Andy called her, she had developed a professional calm that would allow her to be at her best. She went to his office and entered with a slight smile on her lips. "Yes, Andy?"

"Come in. I'm going to take you to Kane's office in a minute, but I want to prep you a little." He had papers spread on his desk.

She pulled up a chair, eager for the details.

It appeared Andy had done a lot of preparation work on the budget and had set up the books.

"Kane wanted me to take this on, but I think you

can do a better job. I did some of the preliminary work, of course, but you'll be able to go on site and verify a lot. It's just across the street, you know.''

''Doesn't Mr. Waterton have a foreman who would take care of some of this?'' Sharon asked.

''He used us last time because he had two projects going at once. Now he has several more projects going, that his own man is working on, but this opportunity came up. Besides, he has some questions about things his guy has done recently. This project is important to him. It's big, Sharon.''

Yes, she could see that. And if he didn't trust his man, she could understand why he wouldn't want him on this project. But why not fire him?

Mr. Waterton would be a strange developer and builder if he was too shy to handle personnel. She couldn't wait to meet him.

Andy indicated they were ready, and she followed him out of his office. She gave a prayer of thanks that they were on the same floor as Kane Haley's office. Since Andy was in a wheelchair, he wouldn't be able to take the stairs, as she always did between their three floors, and she didn't want to arrive at such an important meeting with her wits scattered and her appearance less than professional.

When they reached Maggie's office, she warned them that Kane wasn't ready for them yet, and asked them to wait, indicating the comfortable sofa and chairs near her desk.

That was nothing unusual. Sharon took the sofa and Andy rolled his chair alongside her.

"You're not nervous, are you?" Andy asked, like a mother hen hovering over her only chick.

"Not yet, Andy. I feel well-prepared for this job. Besides, if I find a problem, I can always bring it to you, can't I? You're not going to refuse to speak to me, are you?"

He chuckled. "You know I won't. And Mr. Waterton is a good man to work for. I like him."

A roar of laughter interrupted them, and they both looked at the closed door.

Maggie, with a smile, said, "Kane likes him, too. I think they're becoming true friends."

Sharon automatically smiled, but a frown replaced it as something in the two voices, fainter now but still audible, made her pause.

"What did you say Mr. Waterton's first name was, Maggie?" she asked.

"It's John," Andy answered instead. "I told you that."

"Oh, yes, right," she agreed, still worried.

"But he usually asks everyone to call him—" Maggie began to add, when the door behind her opened.

"There you are," Kane called out, obviously feeling good. "Andrew Huffman, Sharon Davies, I'd like you to meet Jack Waterton."

Jack. The Jack of her dreams. The father-of-her-baby Jack. Thank God she was already sitting down.

Jack Waterton liked his association with Kane Haley. His company was up and coming and eager to please. He'd talked on the phone to Andrew Huffman and liked what he'd heard. Now they wanted him to work with a woman, but he didn't have a problem with that.

He stepped forward and shook Huffman's hand. They'd worked together before. He was a sharp man.

Then he turned to greet the woman. Very attractive, his mind thought, and he felt his body following the same line. His reaction wasn't abnormal for most men. The brunette had long, light brown hair dancing about shoulders that topped a trim figure hidden behind her conservative dress. At least she wasn't a siren.

He smiled and offered her his hand.

And saw her eyes.

Pale green. An unusual color. One that he'd seen in his dreams. Because they were the eyes of the mysterious Sharon. The one who'd disappeared after they'd been trapped in the elevator.

She stood and took his hand for a brisk shake. Then she stepped back, as if she didn't like to touch him.

"Mr. Waterton," she said stiffly.

"Make it Jack, Miss Davies," he said in a friendly manner.

Kane slapped him on the back. "Of course she will, and you'll call her Sharon. We're casual around here."

"Sharon?" he repeated, coming to a sudden halt. The woman in the elevator had had her hair pulled back into a bun. Had she been hiding all that silky hair that framed Sharon's face? Could they be one and the same?

"Come on into the office. Jack has a few problems

he'd like us all to discuss before he and Sharon settle in to detail the project,'' Kane invited, standing back so they could all precede him.

Jack stared at the woman as she walked past him, cool as ice, never looking his way. It couldn't be her. Surely she would've said something...well, maybe not. After all, what happened had been extraordinary and personal. Very personal. So personal that he hadn't been able to forget it.

He dated, sort of, occasionally. Or maybe he should say he had liaisons. But the women always understood the nature of their relationships. He didn't lead anyone on. He'd married once, and he didn't intend to do so again.

Not that he'd led Sharon on in the elevator. She was frightened and panicky, and he'd tried to help her. He hadn't intended to—no, he didn't lose control with women anymore.

But he had that time.

And then she'd walked away.

Had it been a trap? Had she known who he was after all? Maybe she wasn't as innocent as he'd thought her. She couldn't have predicted that the elevator would stick. But it wouldn't be the first time that some fast-thinking woman had used unexpected circumstances to trap a man into thinking with something other than his brain.

"Jack?" Kane prodded him with his voice. "You okay? Ready to talk?"

"Uh, yeah, sure." He turned and followed the others into the office. Kane had said the woman had been with his company eight years. If she started just after college, that would make her thirty. She didn't seem that experienced. In fact, in the elevator, if that was her, he'd thought she was probably twenty. Which left him feeling very guilty. After all, he was thirty-five, considerably older.

He eyed her again as he took a seat across from her. She couldn't be thirty. Her skin was fresh and…and silky, he remembered, warm to his touch. Her lips were warm, too, luscious, blooming under his, and her body—he shook himself. Many more thoughts like that and he'd have to excuse himself.

In his dreams, he'd made love to her in a soft bed, both of them completely naked, able to take the time to enjoy each other. To repeat the loving, again and again. To—

"Mr. Waterton," she began, her voice several degrees beyond frozen.

"Jack, please," he said automatically.

"If you're uncomfortable working with a woman, there are several men in our department who could handle—"

She didn't get her offer completed before both Huffman and Kane objected.

"What are you saying, Sharon?" Huffman asked.

"Are you having second thoughts, Sharon?" Kane wanted to know.

"No, but I believe Mr. Waterton is."

Oho. So she thought she could read his mind? Not likely, or she'd be beet-red from embarrassment. "Forgive me, Sharon. I was momentarily distracted. I have no problem working with you. And my men will be ecstatic when you visit the job."

"I beg your pardon?" she returned, in even icier tones.

Jack shrugged his shoulders. "Am I being politically incorrect by noticing how beautiful you are? Don't worry, my men won't embarrass either you or me." At least not if he threatened them. He cleared his throat. "Shall we get down to business?"

He picked up some papers he'd left nearby that Huffman had prepared. He had a few adjustments to make. He noted that Sharon, woman-in-the-elevator Sharon, had her pen ready and made careful notes as he talked. Andy, as he had asked to be called, made several suggestions, but Sharon amended one of those, improving it. She wasn't afraid to put forth her ideas.

Good for her. Good for him. She'd do a good job...if she didn't drive him crazy.

When they'd covered all the problems he could foresee right now, Kane wished them all luck and escorted them out of his office.

Jack looked at the other two. "How about I buy both of you a cup of coffee? My throat's kind of dry."

"That's a good idea," Andy agreed.

Andy wasn't the one he wanted to talk to. He looked at Sharon for her agreement.

"I really need to get back to the office but you two go right ahead," she said with a small smile directed to her boss.

"Nonsense," Andy corrected. "You work too hard and it's important to get to know a client. We'll both join you, Jack."

Jack was impressed with how quickly she recovered, but he'd caught the frustration and distaste in those remarkable eyes.

"Of course. Go ahead. I'll stop by the office and leave this material. Then I'll meet you there."

Without waiting for a reply, she circled him and Andy and walked out of the office.

Jack led the way to the elevator.

"I'm glad we've got a minute alone," Andy said as the two of them entered an empty elevator.

"Oh, why?"

"You worried me with your remark about her beauty. It's not going to be a problem, is it? I mean, you're aware of the sexual harassment laws, aren't you?"

Jack gave the man a rueful, lopsided grin. "Yeah, I'm aware of them. I was momentarily overcome, she's so damned beautiful, but I'll be careful. You don't have to worry about your baby."

Andy chuckled. "I guess I was pretty transparent," he admitted as the elevator door opened on fifteen and they got out. "But she's worked for me since she got out of high school, and I'm protective of her."

"High school? I thought she had a degree." She might be beautiful, she might fill his dreams, but he expected a certain level of competence.

"She has her degree. She earned it at night while she worked here during the day. She has both experience and training, Jack. She's the best I've got."

Jack nodded. "With an endorsement like that, Andy, how can I go wrong?"

The man nodded in satisfaction as Jack opened the door to the cafeteria so Andy could roll in.

"You can't, Jack. She'll do a good job. Very detail-oriented."

"You've convinced me. By the way, your prep work was quite impressive, too. If things turn out the way I think, I may turn over all my accounting work to Kane Haley, Inc."

"Your suspicions are confirmed?"

"Not yet, but, unfortunately, I believe they will be. I guess the temptation was too great for Roger. I pay him a good salary, but he wanted more. I believe he's falsifying the amounts and skimming. I just can't prove it yet."

"I'm sorry to hear that."

"Yeah. How about here? There's room for your chair at this table. I'll go get the coffee."

He brought two cups back and was turning to go back for a third when Sharon appeared. It startled him when his heart seemed to leap with pleasure. It was those dreams, nothing more. "Sit down, Sharon. I'll go get the third cup."

"No, thank you. I'll have fruit juice." As he turned to discover the location of juice, she added, "I'll get it myself. Go ahead and drink your coffee before it gets cold."

She left before he could argue with her. "Is she always this independent?"

"Yes, she is. And did I mention hard-working?"

"You've sold her, Andy, I promise," he told the man with a grin.

Andy gave him a serene smile. "Good."

Sharon took a long time to get her juice, but she finally joined them. As she sat down, the loudspeaker announced, "Mr. Huffman, you have an important phone call."

Jack watched her eyes widen in apprehension, so he wasn't surprised when she offered to take the phone call for her boss.

"No, I'll get it. You two go ahead and get acquainted." Andy rolled toward the door to the cafeteria. Sharon watched him go as if she'd just lost her best friend.

Jack waited until she faced him again. Then he got straight to the point, afraid she'd run away before he did. And took hold of her arm to be sure. "We need to talk."

Chapter Three

Sharon wasn't sure he'd recognized her, until he touched her. Until he demanded they talk. But she'd had several minutes, while she went to her office, then trodden the steps down to the cafeteria, to figure out her response, in case he had.

"No, we don't. We're going to work together, and I think we can do that. Nothing else matters." She'd practiced those words in her mind as she'd used the stairs. They weren't quite as formal as she'd hoped, but she thought he'd get the point.

Besides, the man hadn't even recognized her. What did it matter to him?

"Sharon, I didn't know where to find you."

Oh, yeah, like he'd cared. "The hospital would've been a good place to start looking." She wasn't going to let him think for a minute that she believed the concern in his voice.

"If you expected me to look for you, why did you leave without finding me?"

"Because, according to the nurse, you'd already left."

"That's what they told me about you." His thumb, resting against the skin on her wrist, began moving in slow circles, all too reminiscent of his attempts to calm her in the elevator, and she jerked her arm away.

"I was there for three hours. I had a cut on my arm that needed a couple of stitches and they were busy." Let him chew on that. She was pretty sure the best he'd had were bruises that required no care.

"You were cut?" he demanded, alarm in his voice.

"Stop it!" she said, louder than she intended, causing several people to turn and stare at them. If Kane Haley heard that she'd upset his biggest client, she'd be out of a job so fast, her head would spin. "Please, Mr. Waterton. I need my job. If we can keep everything on a professional level, I promise I'll handle your work as you wish."

"You think I'd have you fired? Don't be ridiculous, I'd never—"

"If Mr. Haley thought you were displeased—"

"Oh come on, he's not a tyrant. He's a very reasonable man."

Sharon briefly closed her eyes. Of course, he was. But she knew how important this job was to him. And to her. She gathered her strength and looked at him. "I'll do a good job. Now, if you'll give me twenty-four hours, I'll have all the adjustments made and ready to go. Shall I bring them to your office tomorrow?" She prayed he'd follow her lead.

After a determined stare, he sighed and said, "No, I'll stop by your office tomorrow. Or we could have a working lunch?"

"No, thank you. I work better in the office." She stood. "Perhaps you could come by after you have lunch tomorrow, to be sure I get everything done."

"Yes, ma'am. Are you leaving before Andy gets back?"

"Andy's phone calls are never short, Mr. Waterton. I'll let him know our coffee break is over."

"Jack," he said forcefully. The least you can do is call me Jack."

"Of course, Mr.—Jack. Tomorrow." Then she walked out of the cafeteria—and sagged against the wall when she was out of sight.

Now what was he supposed to do? He'd intended to apologize for—for making love to her? Hardly. He didn't regret that. The loving had been the sweetest he'd ever experienced. Probably because of the adrenaline the danger had evoked.

But he hadn't been able to forget it.

His sister had picked him up from the hospital and taken him to his condo because he had a flight out of Chicago that night. His parents had invited both him and his sister and her husband to visit them in Florida to discuss several investments they'd made and the new will they'd drawn up.

He hadn't wanted to go, but his sister had convinced him they should. She had more faith in their parents' love for the two of them than he did. It seemed to him that parents who loved their children wouldn't leave them with nannies and baby-sitters all the time.

Anyway, he'd made his way in life. He was the sole owner of John Waterton Development Company, and it was in good shape. He didn't want his parents' money.

After those two weeks, he'd figured he'd need a reward for the suffering, and he'd lined up a deep-sea fishing trip with friends from college. He'd relaxed on the boat, letting the waves rock him, thinking about Sharon.

If, as he'd assumed, she was an innocent, swept up by the panic and fear she'd exhibited, he'd taken advantage of her. He'd thought about calling the hospital and asking them to check their records. But then he'd told himself he'd check with them when he got back.

Then this project had come up and he'd gotten swept up in it. At night, when he crawled into bed, he thought of Sharon. Thought. Yeah, dreamed, yearned for, craved. But come morning, he was back in the real world, running as fast as he could.

And there was Roger. He had been hurt by the man's betrayal as well as angered. They'd worked together for over ten years. He'd thought they were friends.

Anyway, he'd neglected to make amends.

Then, today, he finds she's his accountant. It all seemed a little coincidental, suddenly. A beautiful woman as a bean counter? Unexpected. A beautiful woman as *his* bean counter, one he'd made love to in an elevator. Unbelievable.

"Where's Sharon?" Andy asked, startling him.

He looked up to find the man had resumed his place at the table. "Hi, Andy. Want me to freshen your coffee?"

"No, thanks. Is everything all right?"

Jack couldn't help but smile. There was that hovering again. "Quit worrying. I didn't scare her away. I'm not even sure that would be possible. She offered to have all the changes in place by tomorrow afternoon and offered to bring them to my office. But I'll be out, so you'll see me here tomorrow. Okay?"

"I told you she was good. She works too hard, though."

"You mean she doesn't slack off when she has a hot date the night before?" He hoped he might pry more information out of Andy than he'd gotten out of Sharon. Which wouldn't be hard since he'd gotten nil from her.

"Nope, not even then."

"What happens if she marries? Will she keep working?"

Andy raised one brow and stared at him. "I don't think she's that involved with anyone at the moment, so I don't think you have to worry about that."

"Oh, good."

"Are you married?"

He stared at Andy, surprised by the question. "No, I'm not."

"Good," Andy said with that serene smile that was beginning to irritate Jack. Then he added, his smile widening, "Just wanted to give as good as I got."

"Sorry. She wasn't very interested in casual chit-chat. It worried me that she was so—so closed up."

"Sharon doesn't make friends easily, but once she does learn to trust someone, they've got a friend for life." Andy pushed his chair back from the table. "Well, I'd best get back to my office and take care of the latest emergency. Let me know if you have any problems with the project."

"I will, Andy, thanks." He stood and shook the man's hand. Then he followed him from the room.

It irritated Sharon, but she put more thought into her appearance the next day than she usually did.

"He's just a lousy man. What's wrong with you?" she asked the image in the mirror. "One who took what he wanted and then walked away. He's not worth any extra primping!"

She twitched her skirt into place and turned to see how much leg she showed through the kick pleat in the back. Obviously her body wasn't listening to her head.

No wonder. Her dreams last night had been even more spectacular than ever. She'd been shocked—when she'd awakened. In her dream she'd been warm and welcoming, begging for his touch. "You idiot!" she snapped, then sighed.

There was no need to worry. He wanted nothing to do with her. If he had, he would've found her. It had been two months. Strictly business. That's what she had to keep in mind.

At work, she kept her mind focused on business. Jack's papers were in order and ready to be shown by ten o'clock. Tidying her desk, she decided she needed a coffee break, or juice break, as she had now decided. She'd read all the material the doctor had given her. One cup of coffee a day was all she should have.

Maybe she was doing overkill, but she'd switched to hot tea at home. Juice for break. Lots of water. And she was discovering some discomfort in her normal suits. Several were a little tight around the waist.

She thought about Jen again. She was seven months, but she'd hidden her condition until almost five months. She needed to ask her for tips, but then she'd have to tell her why. She wasn't ready for that yet.

She stared at the papers she'd neatly stacked there. How long would the project last? She didn't want Jack to know about the baby. She hadn't changed her mind about that.

When she reached the cafeteria, her friends were all there. Julia Parker had joined Maggie, Lauren and Jen. They'd all started about the same time and had gradually formed their own little club. "Am I late?" she asked as she slipped into the last chair.

"Of course not," Maggie assured her. "I was just telling them about your good fortune. Sorry, I should've waited for you to tell them, but they were asking who the hunk was from yesterday."

"The hunk?" she asked, staring at them blankly.

"Oh, come on, Sharon. In the cafeteria yesterday morning. You know, tall, dark, muscles out the wazoo, the most beautiful blue eyes," Julia said.

"My, you certainly took inventory," Sharon said, trying to smile. "And you didn't get his social security number?"

"Do I need it? I had in mind a romantic evening, not retirement."

Everyone laughed, and Sharon said, "Obviously Maggie has told you his name is Jack Waterton. We were talking business, Julia, so I don't know his social details at all."

"Girl, you're going to end up an old maid if you don't start paying attention," Lauren assured her. "We all thought he was well worth a second look."

"You can have one this afternoon. He's coming back after lunch." She hadn't been able to think of anything else all morning.

"Ah, is that why you're wearing a new suit?" Jen asked, grinning.

"It's not new!" Sharon hurriedly assured her. "I bought it two years ago, but then I lost some weight and it didn't fit right. But I'm afraid I've put back on some pounds. Maybe it's the fruit drink," she said, holding up the glass of orange juice.

"You look fine to me," Maggie said, with a warm smile. "Is your cold going away?"

"You have a cold?" Julia asked, frowning. "I don't hear any signs of it. How long have you had it?"

"Oh, I don't, really. For a couple of days, I thought I was coming down with something. That's all. It's all gone away."

"Good, so when Mr. Waterton asks you to dinner, you won't have to turn him down," Jen said.

Sharon stared at her, her mouth open. She had nothing to say.

"Don't say he wasn't attracted to you," Lauren warned. "I saw him take hold of your arm."

"He's—he's one of those touchy people. You know, the kind that hug you after you've met once. That kind of thing. But I explained that I'm not." She tried to take a deep breath without anyone noticing. This coffee break was not relaxing.

"Did he take offense?" Julia asked. "I doubt he gets that response from most women."

Sharon looked at Julia but didn't say anything. She couldn't deny her friend's assessment. That certainly hadn't been her response in the elevator. His arms had been her shelter, her protector.

"Quit teasing Sharon," Maggie ordered. "She knows better than to have a—a social relationship with the man. She's going to be working with him. And it's very important that things go well."

"We won't be working with him," Julia pointed out.

Maggie shook her head and rolled her eyes at Julia. "Go for it, then. I certainly have no intention of stopping you."

"Not me. If I wanted a man, he'd be great, but I'm off men right now."

"Yeah, who isn't?" Sharon muttered and then took a sip of juice. She tried to ignore the pang in her heart. She didn't want him. Not at all. Too bad Julia didn't. She was a beautiful woman, tall, graceful. A lot of fun, too. She'd be perfect for Jack.

She needed a change of subject. "Any word on the child-care center? I'm supposed to check with Michelle by phone before she comes back on Monday. I don't want to get her hopes up if nothing is going to come of it."

"Is Michelle coming back soon? How's her

baby?'' Jen asked. Several others asked about her, too.

It was Maggie who answered her question. ''Kane hasn't changed his mind, if that's what you mean. In fact, he's dedicating more time to it than anything else on his agenda.''

''He's so cute,'' Lauren added and everyone stared at her. ''Oh, I don't mean—well, I do actually. He came to my department and asked about pregnancies—recent ones. He got all embarrassed and half the department wanted to volunteer to get pregnant if he'd be the father.'' She giggled. ''Fortunately, no one told him that.''

''But I gave him a list,'' Maggie said, a question in her eye.

''Yeah, he told Andy he thought maybe some women didn't report their pregnancies right away,'' Sharon said. She'd chosen the topic, but she wasn't feeling much more comfortable with it than she had the first one.

The others looked at Jen.

''Think he's thinking about you, girlfriend?'' Lauren asked her.

''Maybe, but I had a good reason.''

''He said he wanted to know all the pregnancies because the number would affect the decision on whether to have a child-care facility or not,'' Sharon added.

''Well,'' Jen said after some consideration, ''since I'm on the committee, I can understand that, but all those with children under the age of six are being counted, too. So it's not just pregnant women.''

''Say,'' Julia suddenly asked. ''Did you see that

movie I told you about last weekend? There was a pregnant woman in it, and it was a scream.''

The talk turned to movies and Sharon breathed a sigh of relief.

Jack couldn't believe how nervous he was about seeing Sharon this afternoon. He hadn't even eaten much lunch, and usually his appetite could be counted on.

Of course, it could partly be blamed on Roger. He'd joined him for lunch, having just heard that Jack had hired Haley's company for the new project. Jack had given him excuses for the choice, but he had a feeling Roger wasn't satisfied.

He would've preferred lunch with Sharon.

He straightened his tie and stepped out of the elevator on the sixteenth floor. Sometimes he didn't wear a tie, especially when most of his day was spent on the job. His men would laugh at him. But it was important that he look his best for Sharon. To help her stick to business. Like she wanted.

Him, too. That's what he wanted. Then he chuckled at that blatant lie.

When he reached Sharon's desk, he was able to stare at her without her being aware because of the woman sitting on the corner of her desk, chatting.

She looked wonderful today, the dark green suit picking up a touch of red-gold in her long hair.

"Excuse me?" he said softly before he could get too wrapped up in her appearance. That wasn't safe.

Sharon jumped, apparently startled.

"I didn't mean to scare you, Sharon. Shall I wait in the hallway, or—''

"Oh, no, of course not, Mr. Waterton!" she exclaimed, her voice sounding stressed.

"Jack, remember?"

"Yes, um," Her teeth nibbled her bottom lip and he wanted to join in.

The woman with Sharon stood and held out a hand. "I'm Deedee West. I apologize for keeping you waiting."

"No problem. If you need more time—"

"No, not at all. I had tickets for the new show at the Art Institute and thought Sharon might go, but she can't." The woman looked at him with a practiced air of sophistication and leaned closer. "I don't suppose you'd be interested in going?"

He'd been hit on before. But his mind was completely on Sharon. "Uh, no, thank you. It's a busy time for me."

"Well, if you change your mind, I'm in the department across the hall." She took a card from her pocket and slid it into Jack's breast pocket. "Give me a call."

Jack smiled, having collected himself. "Thank you. I'll remember." The heck of it was she was the kind of lady he enjoyed. Someone who knew the score. Sophisticated, not clingy.

But he immediately turned to Sharon, no regrets in his mind. "Shall I find a chair or—"

"We can talk in the conference room. The table's large and we can spread out the papers," she replied, standing to lead the way.

He loved following her. Her trim hips had an enchanting swing that mesmerized him. He jerked his gaze to her face when she opened the door and swung around to face him.

He grinned at her, inviting her to share his pleasure, but she frowned. "Is anything wrong?"

"No, of course not," he assured her. "Shall I close the door?"

Panic seemed to fill her eyes. Then she gave him a brief smile. "No. We won't be interrupted."

So, she didn't trust him.

It didn't take all that long to go over the setup. She'd done a good job of getting everything ready. If, on occasion, he brushed against her arm, or leaned in closer to check things out, he noticed her withdrawal, but it wasn't that obvious. He didn't think an outsider would be aware of it.

Did that mean she wasn't as calm as she pretended to be? Was she that good an actor? In the elevator, she hadn't been calm about anything. Even before the elevator stopped, she'd been tense.

"Jack? Did you have a question about this item?"

He looked up, startled. "Why, no. Did you think I did? You did a wonderful job on the preparation."

"Thank you," she murmured and began gathering up the papers, obviously considering the conversation to be finished.

"There's just one thing."

She immediately tensed. "Yes?"

"I'd like to show you over the site today. You'll need to be a frequent visitor and I want you to be comfortable."

"That can wait, I'm sure," she protested.

"No, it can't."

He watched the struggle on her face. Then, that

professional demeanor she'd been exhibiting took over.

"Of course, Mr. Waterton. I'll drop these papers back by my desk and let Andy know."

"Good, but you're supposed to call me Jack."

His easy smile didn't seem to have an effect on her.

"It seemed a bit forward to call you Jack when you're cracking the whip." Then she turned and left the conference room.

He hurried after her. Okay, so maybe he'd sounded more like a road boss than someone extending an invitation. But he *was* the boss. For now.

When she was ready, he led the way to the elevators. It wasn't until he'd pushed the button and turned to make a polite remark, that he realized there was a problem.

Sharon's face was white as the elevator doors slid open. Before he could reach out to her, he looked over his shoulder to discover the elevator was the first on the left. The same elevator in which they'd spent a number of hours together.

Retching sounds had him spinning around again, reaching for his handkerchief, as Sharon became ill.

"Oh, hell," he muttered.

Chapter Four

Sharon was totally humiliated.

Jack wrapped his arms around her and wiped her face with his handkerchief.

"I—I'm sorry," she managed as she straightened and tried to put some distance between them. The warmth of his embrace reminded her too much of their time in the elevator. He could convince a woman surrounded by attackers that she was totally safe if he held her.

"Take it easy. You're fine." He paused, still holding on to her, then said, "At least, I hope you are. Let's go back in the department where we can find you a chair."

He helped her through the door of her department and Alice, an older lady, motherly, leaped to her feet and ran toward them. "What happened to Sharon?"

"She's feeling ill."

Sharon was delighted to exchange Jack's care for Alice's. Alice didn't make her pulse go crazy. Or fill her dreams. "Alice, would you go with me to the ladies' room?"

"Of course, honey," Alice said, leading her away from Jack. Once they were in the ladies' room, Sharon fell onto the sofa, resting her head on its cushions.

"What can I do for you? Do you have the flu?"

Sharon was tempted by that total lie, but she decided to use a half-truth instead. "No, but it's been a tense day and the elevator—I just couldn't handle it."

"Oh, you poor dear, of course. If that had happened to me, I don't think I could've gotten in one again. Shall I go to the cafeteria and get you a soda to settle your stomach?"

"That would be so nice, Alice. But could you stop by the department and tell Mr. Waterton I'll meet him tomorrow morning at his project at whatever time he wants." Hopefully, that would take him away before she had to leave the safety of the ladies' room.

"Of course I will, dear." Alice bustled out, leaving Sharon in blessed silence.

She closed her eyes, drawing deep breaths, glad her stomach appeared to be settled now. So far, she hadn't suffered from morning sickness, just a general queasiness. She'd just received a warning, however, that if she didn't remain calm, she might suffer more.

For the first time since her visit to the doctor, she truly felt pregnant. She recognized that her body was changing.

Her hand crept across her stomach, still flat. "I'll keep you safe," she whispered.

She would. Tonight she'd tell her mother about the change in her life and she'd start making preparations for the future. It was time to get over the shock.

Jack was standing there, feeling helpless, when Andy rolled out of his office.

"What's going on? Where are Alice and Sharon going?" the man asked.

"Uh, Sharon got sick and Alice is helping her."

"Sick?"

"I think she's still nervous about the elevator after, you know, being trapped." He ran his hand through his hair. He wanted to know if she was all right, but he couldn't follow them to the ladies' room.

"She told you about that?"

Alarm bells suddenly went off. To Jack's surprise, the press hadn't gotten hold of the story about the elevator, and he'd forgotten that no one knew of his involvement. "Uh, yeah, it came up."

Andy studied him, making him a little nervous. "That's surprising. She seldom talks about it. I didn't realize it still bothered her."

"Should someone go after them to see if she needs a doctor?" Jack asked, ignoring Andy's words.

"No, I—" Andy began, but he stopped because he saw Alice in the hall. "Here's Alice."

"How's Sharon?" Jack demanded, stepping forward.

"She's fine. I'm going to get her a soda, Andy. I'll

be back in a minute. Oh, you'd better call a janitor to tidy up the foyer.''

''I will. Are you sure she's okay?'' Andy asked.

''Yes. And Mr. Waterton, she said she'd meet you at the site in the morning at whatever time you say.'' She smiled and stood waiting.

He stared at her. What was she waiting for?

''What time shall I tell her?'' Alice finally said.

''I don't know. I'll hang around until she's better and we'll—we'll work out a time.'' He shoved his hands in his pockets and leaned against the wall, imitating a permanent fixture.

Alice looked at Andy. Jack thought something was being communicated, but he wasn't sure what.

Andy wheeled around and ordered one of his employees to call the janitor. Then he faced Jack again. ''I wouldn't waste my time waiting, Jack. Women can be slow about these things. And it's only half an hour till quitting time.''

''I don't need to get back for anything,'' Jack assured him. ''Maybe she just needs a good meal. I'll take her out to dinner. That will make her feel better.''

Andy looked him in the eye. ''That's thoughtful of you, Jack, but I think Sharon may not feel like eating dinner.''

Jack frowned, debating his options. He wanted to see Sharon, to be sure she was all right. His gut told him this sickness was important. But he couldn't insist she go to dinner. Especially not with Andy hovering over them.

He reached in his pocket and pulled out a business

card. Turning it over, he wrote his home number on the back. "Here's my home number. When she gets home, she can call me and we'll discuss the best time."

"I'll give her the message," Andy said, a genial smile on his face. "Thanks for being so understanding."

Understanding? Hell, he was frustrated. But Andy had him boxed in and they both knew it. He nodded and stomped out of the department back to the dreaded elevators.

After Alice brought her the soda and reported that Mr. Waterton had apparently left without setting a time, Sharon was ready to return to her desk. She needed to figure out what to do about tomorrow.

Several of her co-workers asked about her health when she and Alice got back to the office, and she assured them she was fine. She'd no more than sat down when her phone rang and Andy asked her to come to his office.

She should've known. He was even more motherly than Alice, and she'd told Sharon that he'd asked about her.

She walked into his office. "I'm fine, Andy. I must've eaten something bad at lunch."

"Really? Jack thought it was your fear of elevators."

Sharon stared at him, her mind working frantically for a reasonable answer.

"Do you and Jack have a—a relationship?" Andy asked.

Sharon took a chair, releasing a deep sigh. Time for another half-truth. "Uh, Andy, the truth is—well, you see—"

"Sharon, if you're dating him, you should've told me before now." Andy looked as severe as he could.

"No! I would've—that is, I'm not dating anyone. But—but he was the man trapped in the elevator with me," she finally said with a rush.

Andy stared at her, his mouth dropping open. Then he said, "Why didn't you tell me when I first brought up his name?"

"Because I didn't *know* his name. All I knew was Jack. And I hadn't seen him since that day."

"Why didn't he recognize you when we went into Kane's office?"

"I had my hair pulled back, so I looked different. And we spent most of those hours in the dark. He probably would've recognized my voice if I'd—anyway, he did figure out who I was eventually, but he didn't say anything until we were alone."

"What did he say?"

"He wanted to talk about it, but I said we should stick to business," she assured him, hoping she'd wipe the frown from his face.

It didn't disappear.

"Discuss it? What's to discuss?"

Sharon prayed for divine intervention, but nothing happened. "Uh, I guess he wanted to—to see if I'd recovered."

"So you answered him by throwing up the first time he takes you near an elevator. Have you been riding the elevators since that incident?"

"Yes, of course. Every morning and every evening."

"Okay. Well, he wanted to wait to be sure you were all right. Thoughtful of him," Andy said, staring at her.

She hoped she hid her dismay. "Yes, very."

"But I convinced him that might take some time, so he left this."

Andy put a white card down on his desk and pushed it toward Sharon. While she reached for it, he explained, "It's his business card. He wrote his home number on the back and asked that you call him this evening to discuss the time that would be best for both of you."

"Call him at home?" Sharon asked, her voice rising.

"Yes. I'd said you'd be glad to. It's not a problem, is it?"

"No, of course not. Is it okay if I go there first, before coming to the office? Then I won't have to ride up twice."

"That's fine. Do you want to see a doctor about riding elevators? I should've offered right away. A psychologist, maybe?"

"No! It was just one incident, Andy. I'm fine."

"Okay, but if you get in trouble, any kind of trouble, you let me know. Do you hear me?"

"I hear you, Papa Bear," Sharon said with a smile.

Alice insisted on riding the elevator with Sharon when she started home, even offering to hold her hand if it would help.

"Thank you, Alice. That's so sweet of you, but I'm really all right. Thank you for taking care of me this afternoon."

"My pleasure. My children have all moved away from home and I miss looking after them," Alice assured her and bid her a cheerful goodnight when they reached the lobby.

Sharon walked to her stop on the El. All the way home, she thought about how she would tell her mother about her pregnancy. There was no simple way.

"Sharon?" her mother called as Sharon opened the front door of their modest suburban home. "You're home early tonight. You usually work several hours of overtime. Is everything all right?"

"Fine, Mom," Sharon said, leaning over to kiss her mother's cheek. Only the two of them lived there now. The second child, Joanie, was married and living in Topeka, Kansas. Her brothers, the twins, had finished school last year and got an apartment together. Evie, the baby, two years younger than the boys, was starting her junior year and living with three other girls near the campus of the University of Illinois.

Sharon had been a little envious, but she'd stayed at home because money had been needed to pay tuitions through the years, hers and her siblings'. Maybe her mother would *want* her to move out when she heard her news.

"Uh, Mom, do you have a minute? We need to talk."

Her mother had already started to the kitchen again.

She stopped and whirled around. "I knew it! Something's wrong, isn't it? Has someone been hurt? Why didn't they call me here? I've been home this afternoon. They called you at work? I don't—"

"Mom," Sharon said firmly, taking her mother's arm. "Calm down. No one's hurt. Come into the kitchen and we'll have a cup of—something to drink." She couldn't have coffee, but she didn't want to point that out to her mother. Not yet.

When they entered the kitchen, her mother immediately reached for cups and saucers, but Sharon put hers back. "I'm having some juice," she said, smiling, and got down a glass.

Her mother stared at her as she poured her coffee, almost letting her cup overflow. "It's you, isn't it? Did you go to the doctor? Do you have cancer?"

"No, I don't—yes, I went to the doctor, but no, I don't have cancer." She'd intended to build up to what she had to say, but she gave up. Her mother was going to suspect all kinds of disasters if she didn't tell her. "Mom," she began, then sighed deeply. "I'm pregnant."

Stunned, her mother fell into a chair at the table, her coffee spilling into the saucer. She said nothing, staring at Sharon.

"I'm sorry I shocked you. I understand if you don't want me to live here anymore. I didn't plan on—"

"Don't be ridiculous! It's just that I didn't know you were dating anyone. Of course you'll stay here till you marry. I wouldn't hear of anything else."

Sharon sighed again. "There won't be a marriage, Mom."

"Some jerk got you pregnant and won't marry you? Who is he? I'll talk to him. He'll change his tune."

Her mother was five foot two and slender as a girl. The thought of her facing Jack Waterton and putting fear in him would've been quite comical. Except that Jack didn't know about their baby…her baby.

"Mom, I haven't told the father."

"Sharon! Surely you weren't dating a married man? Surely I taught you better than that."

"Look, Mom, I'd better explain. Just—just hear me out. Then you can scream at me all you want."

"I wasn't screaming," she protested. When Sharon held up a hand, she subsided in her chair.

"When I was trapped in the elevator, I panicked. The man with me…comforted me. We were alone in the dark for a number of hours and—and I was panicky—and one thing led to another and we had sex!

"I felt so safe in his arms, and so afraid I was going to die. When he touched me I felt alive. I forgot about the danger. I welcomed his advances."

Silence.

"So," Sharon finally continued, "I don't know if he's married. I don't know—" Oops, she'd told herself for so long that she didn't know his last name, she'd forgotten she now did. "He didn't give me his last name."

"But surely you could find it. You could call the hospital. I'm sure—"

"He left the hospital before me. He didn't want anything to do with me in the real world."

"You could at least get child support."

Sharon shrugged her shoulders. "I guess it's more my fault than his. He wasn't having hysterics. Besides, with my new raise, I'll be able to provide for my child."

"What new raise?"

Sharon realized she'd been so overwhelmed with the events of yesterday, she hadn't told her mother the good news. "I was promoted and given a raise."

"That's wonderful," her mother said. "So—so you're going to have your child alone? I didn't want that kind of life for any of you. You know how hard it is."

"But we made it, Mom. Besides, you were still in love with Father, so it was harder for you."

"I'm not anymore."

"I know and I'm glad." Gradually her mother had gotten over her feelings for her husband. Not that she dated a lot—or at all, Sharon thought with a smile.

"Dear, I have something to tell you, too."

In an attempt at humor, Sharon said, "Don't tell me you're pregnant, too!"

"No! Of course not. But—but I'm in love. I met him at church and—and he's very nice. I've wanted to introduce you but I was afraid..."

Though Sharon wasn't at ease with her mother's news, she pulled her into her arms for a hug.

Jack paced the living room of his elegant condo. It had a breathtaking view of the rest of downtown and the lake. A professional decorator, hired by his mother, had decorated it and it was filled with glass and metal and a black-and-white décor.

Very chic, and very not him.

But what had he cared? It was a place to sleep, not much more. Since his wife had died, he hadn't wanted a "nest." She hadn't wanted a nest then. But he'd found a nice house in the suburbs with a yard. So his child could play. She would've loved this condo, but not the house.

But then, she hadn't wanted the child either.

He rubbed the back of his neck as he stopped in front of the floor-to-ceiling window. Hell! They'd been totally wrong for each other, but she'd told him she was pregnant, once she found out how much he was worth. He'd swallowed that lie hook, line and sinker.

Once he realized she wasn't pregnant, he'd been angry, but they were married. He'd made it work. Then not long after she became pregnant for real, she and the baby were gone in the snap of a finger.

He turned to glare at the phone. Why hadn't Sharon called?

He checked his watch again. It was almost seven-thirty. Maybe she'd lost the card. He could call her. That's what he'd do. He'd call her.

Starting for the phone, he came to an abrupt halt. He didn't have her number. Or her address. And he suspected there would be a lot of Davies in the phone book. He did know Kane's number, however.

"Kane? Jack Waterton. You wouldn't happen to have Sharon's home number, would you? We were supposed to talk tonight to set up a meeting tomorrow, and I'm afraid she lost my number."

"No, I don't have it, but I can get it for you. I'll call you right back."

It only took five minutes, but Jack wasn't a patient man. When Kane called, he thanked him and hung up at once, eager to dial the number.

A sweet voice answered the phone, but it wasn't Sharon. He knew he'd have no difficulty recognizing her beautiful tones.

"Is Sharon there?"

"Yes, she is. May I tell her who's calling?"

He didn't want to do that. She might decide not to take the call, but it was only polite to tell her his name.

A couple of minutes later, Sharon picked up the phone.

"Sharon? You hadn't called and I was afraid you'd lost my number." His excuse sounded silly to him, but it was all he could think of.

"I apologize. My mother had—that is, I've been busy. I should have called earlier. Has anything urgent come up?"

"No, but I—I was concerned about your health, too. How are you?"

"Fine, Mr. Waterton. I'm fine."

"Jack, *please*. Did you ride the elevators down?"

"Yes, of course."

She was keeping her answers short and her voice clipped, nothing like the warm tones in the elevator. "Uh, I hope you don't mind that I called."

"No, but how did you get my number?"

"I called Kane."

"Mr. Haley had my number?" she said in surprise.

"No, but he knew where to get it. Want me to call and ask how he got it?"

"No! It doesn't matter. What time tomorrow do you want to meet?"

"I'm flexible. What time's best for you?"

"I'd prefer to meet first thing rather than interrupt my work later. I thought that might be best for you, too."

"Good. I'll buy you breakfast and then—"

"No. No breakfast. Shall we say eight-thirty?"

"What's wrong with breakfast?"

"Nothing, but I prefer not to include social activities in our relationship," she said stiffly.

"Sharon, you're being ridiculous. I already know you."

After a painful silence, she said, "I'll see you at eight-thirty." And she hung up.

Chapter Five

Jack's crew was on the work site at seven the next morning. Most of the men had worked for him for quite some time and he trusted them. They were almost more family than his own family.

Occasionally, his mother or sister would appear at a job site. Once his sister even got out of the car to look at his work. She hurried back to the safety of her vehicle when she realized how dirty it could be. His mother never ventured beyond the open door of her limo to chastise him for not having turned on his cell phone. His father wore exquisite suits and sat in a pristine office dealing stocks and bonds. He had no interest in building things.

Today, Sharon would visit the site. He wanted her to be familiar with the setup and meet his second-in-command. He knew better than to expect any appreciation for what he did. But he couldn't help hoping. Anticipating.

"You okay, boss?" Pete Turley asked. He was the field boss for this crew, the best Jack had.

"Sure. Why do you ask?"

"You seem distracted. The architect wants a word with you." Pete gestured to a man in a dark suit.

"Yeah, okay, but keep a lookout for the accountant."

"Another suit? We're getting a lot of visits this morning." Pete shrugged and turned away.

"Uh, Pete?" Jack called softly. "This one may be wearing a skirt." He grinned at Pete's surprise. "When she gets here, call me at once."

Pete grinned back. "Gotcha, boss."

Jack was still talking to the architect when he saw Sharon appear. She was sensibly dressed in gray trousers with a matching jacket and a cream turtleneck sweater under it. And she looked great. The men hadn't noticed her, which was a good thing. He didn't want any wolf whistles to upset her.

He excused himself from the architect and hurried to the edge of the property where Sharon stood. "Good morning."

"Good morning—Jack. I hope I'm not too early."

"Not at all. Do you mind taking a closer look? It's a little dirty, but—"

"Of course I want a closer look. I see the excavation is done."

"Yeah, I sublet that job. We're laying the foundation now. I want to introduce my field boss in case I'm not here and you have questions." He watched her closely for signs of distaste or disdain, but he saw none.

The small building he'd moved on to the property sat nearby and he led her to it. "I have something for you."

She appeared startled. "I don't think—gifts are not necessary. I'm doing my job."

"And this will help you do it," he assured her. Inside the portable office, he picked up a hard hat. "I didn't giftwrap it," he pointed out, grinning, "but you have to wear it anytime you're on the property."

Across the back of the silver helmet, he'd printed her last name. "That's very nice of you, but I won't be here that often, I'm sure. It's not necessary—"

"Yes, it is. We obey safety rules on my jobs. No exceptions." Then he lifted the helmet and placed it on her light-brown curls. Her femininity was in direct contrast to the masculine helmet, making her look even more tempting.

Jack cleared his throat. "Uh, shall we go find Pete?"

Without comment, she followed him out the door.

"Are you feeling all right this morning?"

She stopped and stared at him. "Why wouldn't I?" she demanded.

Jack frowned. "You threw up yesterday. I wondered if it was the flu instead of the elevator, that's all."

"I'm fine," she replied, her voice brisk.

Pete was on the bottom floor, three levels below them, where the crew was working. The only means of reaching him was by stepping on the cable platform and lowering it. He figured he'd better call Pete up rather than subject Sharon to that descent. After all, if she didn't like elevators, she certainly wouldn't like the small platform. He waved to his lieutenant and motioned him up.

"Aren't we going down?" she asked.

"I was afraid it would upset you."

"It's not closed in, and it's only three stories. I can make it," she assured him, her chin rising.

With a shrug, he motioned to Pete to wait there and helped her on the small platform, keeping his hand on her arm. "Hold on," he ordered, nodding to the safety bar.

She looked pale when they reached the bottom and he felt he'd made a mistake. He should've brought Pete to the top.

Sharon, however, stepped off the lift and extended her hand to Pete, who was waiting for them. "Are you the field boss? I'm Sharon Davies, the bean counter."

Pete's gaze was glued to Sharon's face, his grin widening. "Ma'am," he said with reverence. "You're the prettiest bean counter I've ever seen."

Instead of being offended, as Jack had expected, Sharon took Pete's comment as intended and thanked him nicely. He watched in fascination as Sharon charmed Pete, asking pertinent questions. When one of the men looked up, Sharon extended her hand to him and introduced herself. The man rubbed his hand on his backside before extending it.

Suddenly, every man on the job had business in the area and just happened to stop so he could be introduced to the beautiful woman. Several of them drew her over to particular areas of work so they could show off their expertise. Even the architect, whose meeting had ended, got into the act, offering to show her the blueprints he'd produced.

Jack's plans of having Sharon to himself evaporated. He scarcely got a word in edgewise, following her tamely around his project. But the pride he felt at her adaptation filled him. Had her father been in construction? Was that why she handled the situation so well? He realized how little he knew about her...and yet he'd made love to her. Incredible love.

"Jack?" she called, rousing him from his thoughts.

"Yes?"

"I need to go to my office now unless there's anything else you want me to see."

He couldn't hold back a grin. "I can't think of anything else. You've already seen more than I had in mind."

"I'm sorry if I took too much of your time," she hurriedly said, her cheeks flushing.

"Don't be ridiculous. I'm pleased with your visit. My men certainly will look forward to you appearing." They still were hovering near Sharon, pretending to work, watching her.

"Your crew is a nice bunch. I enjoyed meeting them."

Several men grinned, telling Jack they'd overheard her words.

"Now I can put names with faces when I do the payroll," she added, smiling at those closest to her.

Jack decided he'd better get her out of there before everyone invited her back every day, and no work got done. "Ready?" he asked, gesturing to the lift.

She wasn't quite as eager to get on the lift this time, and Jack faced her when he stepped on with her. "Keep your eyes on me and tell me what you think of the project. We'll be on top in no time."

To his surprise, she did as he asked, but the words didn't flow as they had below. Maybe it was the elevator, or maybe it was him. He didn't know.

"I—I think you're off to a good start. P-Pete seems easy to work with and—and your men were very welcoming."

Having kept his hand on her arm, he now guided her steps to solid ground. "Good job, Sharon."

With a cautious look down, she quickly turned away. "Thank you." She took off her helmet, but he stopped her and put it back on her head.

"Not until you get to the office, my office," he hurriedly added. "And anytime you come on the property, that's your first stop. Promise?"

"Yes, of course."

"Good. Now, how about a cup of coffee to relax. You seem a little tense."

"No, thank you, I have to return to the office."

Was "no" always the first word out of her mouth? Did she never relax? He was getting more than a little irritated with her standoffishness.

"I have to visit Kane, so I'll come to your cafeteria for the coffee…or fruit juice or whatever you want. That's a compromise, lady, and I recommend you accept it."

He hadn't meant to sound like a growly bear. But he was used to getting his own way.

She stared at him, her gaze reflecting the irritation

he was feeling. At least she wasn't ignoring him. He held her gaze, not backing down.

"Very well," she snapped. "I'll see if Andy can join us."

"Fine!" he snapped in return. Then, having reached the temporary office, he took her hard hat from her and stuck it inside. "Let's go."

"Mr. Waterton, I can find my way without your guidance," she assured him, her tones frigid as she stared at his hand on her arm.

"I'm sure you could, Miss Davies, but *I* might get lost." At that blatant lie, all conversation stopped, but he kept his hand on her arm. He liked touching her. Even through her jacket and sweater. Their bodies made a connection even if she resisted their association.

He'd questioned his behavior in the elevator that first day, the day he made love to her. He was a disciplined man. He didn't give in to his sexual urges at the drop of a hat. But that day—holding her in his arms, trying to care for her, to keep her safe, the connection had been so fierce, so special, he'd let himself do what he shouldn't have. She was so much younger than him.

Which reminded him. "How old are you?"

"I beg your pardon?" she asked. They'd just crossed the street and she came to an abrupt halt on the corner. Glaring up at him, she asked, "Why would you ask me that question?"

"Because you look so damn young."

"I'm twenty-five, Mr. Waterton, and I know my job!"

"I wasn't complaining. I just needed to know."

He remembered her telling him, as they'd lain together, about trying to ensure that her siblings all got their college degrees. He'd assumed she'd gotten hers first. But Andy told him she went to school at night and worked all day.

He wasn't sure his sister would even return a phone call to him, unless it was in her best interest. He knew his mother wouldn't. His father? He'd never called him at work. That was forbidden. He was too busy.

They entered the lobby of Sharon's building. The door of "their" elevator stood open, and he felt a sudden tug on his hand as she came to an abrupt halt. "You go on up. I'll—stop off here for a moment," she said, nodding her head toward the public rest rooms to one side.

"Are you feeling sick again?"

"No! But I—I don't take *that* elevator," she confessed, her voice very low, so he had to bend toward her to hear the words.

Before he could respond, the elevator doors closed and the second elevator opened up.

"Okay, we can go up now," she suddenly said and bolted for the new elevator, leaving him behind.

He hurried after her.

Sharon hadn't wanted to face both the elevator ride and Jack together. Too many memories. She closed her eyes and tried to think of something to distract her. She almost jumped out of her shoes when Jack's strong arm came around her shoulders.

Her eyes popped open and she stared at him. "What are you doing?"

"Helping you get through this," he said, frowning.

"No, thank you," she ripped back, stepping away from him and shoving his arm away. "What if some-one saw us? They'd think you were—were—"

"Coming on to you? Having an affair with you?"

"Yes! Either of those things!"

"Neither of us is married. What's wrong with that?"

She gaped at him. "It's unprofessional! I'd prob-ably lose my job!"

The elevator door slid open and she rushed out. She'd punched sixteen, not fifteen where the cafeteria was. "I have to stop by the office. You could go on to the cafeteria—"

"No."

Without any other words to soften his answer, he followed her into the department. To her frustration, he greeted Alice with a smile and thanked her again for assisting Sharon the evening before.

"Oh, I didn't mind at all. Sharon is such a dear," Alice said, beaming.

"I couldn't agree more," Jack said with a friendly nod that set Sharon's teeth on edge.

"Is Andy in?" Sharon asked.

"Oh, no, dear, he had to go to a meeting. Lillian called him a few minutes ago," Alice said and winked at Sharon.

Sharon couldn't hold back a smile. Everyone knew Lillian, a lady about Alice's age in Accounts Payable, had a crush on Andy. She looked for reasons to see him during the workday. But Sharon had wanted Andy to join them for their break so she wouldn't be alone with Jack.

"Tell him we'd like him to join us if he gets back any time soon, please, Alice." She ignored Jack's face, not wanting to see his reaction.

"I will, dear," Alice agreed with a happy nod.

Then Sharon had no choice but to look at Jack. "Ready?"

"After you."

She didn't hesitate to lead him to the stairs. No more elevators for her until she went home that evening, thank goodness. They were too hard on her system, especially when Jack was with her.

In the cafeteria, not crowded because it was not quite ten yet, Jack chose a table for them and asked her if she wanted coffee.

"No thanks. I'm going to have a soda." One a day wouldn't hurt her, the doctor had said. And she needed it this morning.

He insisted on buying her soda for her. "I'm the last of the big-time spenders, Sharon," he said dryly, "a whole half-dollar."

"But I should be treating you, Jack. After all, you're my client."

"Ah," he said, a gleam in his eye that worried her. "Then I can expect to be wined and dined occasionally?"

Sharon was completely at a loss. She knew Kane Haley wouldn't hesitate to treat a customer, but she'd never—"I'm sure Mr. Haley will—"

"Aha! I hear my name being used in vain," Kane

exclaimed behind Sharon, shaking her up even more. "Good morning to both of you. How's it going?"

"Mr. Haley!" Sharon exclaimed, turning in her chair.

"Mind if I join you?" he asked, pulling out the chair beside Jack.

Of course, Sharon didn't object. But she wasn't sure Kane Haley being part of the group was any better than being alone with Jack.

Especially when he asked his question. "What is it I'll do, Sharon? You need something?"

She didn't know what to answer. As she considered her options, Jack took over.

"It was my fault, Kane. I think I startled Sharon when I asked if I was going to be wined and dined as a customer."

"Any time you want," Kane agreed, a smile on his face. "In fact, I've got tickets to opening night for the Bulls. We could eat and then catch the game. I'm not promising Michael Jordan-quality ball, but it'd be fun."

"Ringside?" Jack asked, and the two men talked basketball, leaving Sharon time to catch her breath.

"Actually, I was teasing Sharon, because I can't even get her to have breakfast or lunch with me. The best I've managed so far is coffee here. I'm not complaining, Kane, but your break room doesn't have a lot of ambience," Jack said with a grin.

Sharon caught Kane's quick look, which told her she'd be visiting with him later, but she didn't say anything.

Kane then smiled at Jack. "She's an unusual employee, Jack. Likes to keep her nose to the grindstone. How about the Bulls game and dinner to make up for her neglect?''

"Sure, Kane, I'd enjoy it. But if you had other plans for those tickets, don't change your plans for me. I'm well-satisfied with the deal we struck. Sharon visited the site today and charmed my entire crew.''

Kane beamed at him. ''Good for her. And she'll be even better at managing the funds and keeping details. Andy swears she's the best.''

Sharon wanted to hide under the table. Such glowing praise was a bit excessive in her mind.

"I couldn't agree more," Jack said.

She had to get out of there. ''Since you're here to entertain Jack, Mr. Haley, if you don't mind, I'll excuse myself.'' She stood abruptly, and both gentlemen leaped to their feet. ''Oh, sorry, please sit down.''

They ignored her. Kane said, ''Stop by my office sometime this afternoon, Sharon, and, please, call me Kane. You know we're informal here.''

"Yes, sir, of course. I'll check with Maggie for a time.''

"Good idea. You know she's a martinet about my schedule. But I'd be lost without her,'' he added with a smile.

"Yes, sir.'' With a nod in Jack's direction, she started to leave.

"I'll call you later,'' Jack added with a smile.

"Of—of course.'' Just what she wanted. More contact with Jack today. But at least it wouldn't be in an elevator!

* * *

"Did I get her in trouble?" Jack asked abruptly after the two men had sat back down.

"No, of course not. But she's new to being in charge. She doesn't know about expense accounts and extending invitations to our clients. I should've thought of that earlier."

"You should've seen her with my crew today, Kane. They were eating out of her hands. I've never seen anything like it," Jack added, trying to make sure he hadn't done any damage to Sharon's reputation.

"Well, she's a beautiful woman. We men tend to react that way. But, you know, it will be a little awkward—her taking you out as a client. After all, she's new to management duties."

Jack's gaze sharpened on Kane. "What do you mean?"

"It's the man-woman thing. I hadn't really thought about that because my managers are all men except one, and she's married, usually includes her husband."

Jack held up his hands, palms out. "I wouldn't cross the line, Kane. Not on a business dinner. She's beautiful, of course, but I know a lot of beautiful women. I've never had any complaints."

"I know. I didn't mean you'd do something wrong. But it might be better if Andy or I come with the two of you. Just to keep everyone comfortable."

"Or I could invite my mother to play chaperone," Jack added, his voice full of sarcasm.

"Not a bad idea."

Jack leaned back and laughed. "Which proves you've never met my parents."

"No, I haven't, but at least you've got the idea. We men have to be careful in today's world not to give the wrong impression. There've been times when I thought I'd take Maggie to dinner when we're working late. What's the difference between that and ordering in food? But—but we haven't—" He stopped and sighed.

"Yeah, I get the picture, Kane. We'll keep it to a crowd." He smiled at him and picked up his cup and drained it. "Well, I'd better get to work and stop wasting my day," he added, shaking Kane's hand.

It appeared the only place he'd ever be alone with Sharon again was on the elevator. And she wasn't happy about that.

Chapter Six

Maggie scheduled Sharon's conference with Kane at two-fifteen. That made lunch problematical for Sharon because she was afraid to eat. It might come back up at an inopportune moment.

She mentioned her appointment to Andy, and he offered to come with her, but Sharon knew she had to face the music alone. If she wanted the benefits of her promotion, then she had to bear the responsibilities, too. So she turned down Andy's offer.

She reached Maggie's office a few minutes early. "I'm ahead of schedule, Maggie. I didn't want to be late. May I wait here?" she asked, gesturing to the sofa.

"Of course, Sharon. Is everything all right?"

"I'm not sure. I think I mishandled Mr. Waterton today. I was caught off guard. I'm hoping Kane will excuse me on grounds of inexperience rather than incompetence."

Maggie smiled. "He's a fair man."

Sharon smiled in return and breathed deeply. Stay calm, she repeated to herself. The most important thing was the health of her baby.

At two-fifteen, Maggie announced her arrival to Kane, and he stood as Sharon went in. "Close the door, Maggie," he said, then smiled at Sharon.

Taking another deep breath, Sharon remained standing until Kane gestured to one of the chairs in front of his desk. Nice chairs, covered with soft green leather.

"I owe you an apology, Sharon."

Surprised, Sharon gaped at him. "You do?" She cleared her throat so her voice wouldn't sound like a baby bird begging for food. "I mean, I can't think of any reason, sir."

"I didn't prepare you for all your responsibilities, like entertaining the client. I should've made sure you understood that aspect of the job," he said, still smiling.

Was he going to tell her she had to take Jack out for an evening on the town? Sharon wasn't sure she could manage that. Would her promotion, the extra money, disappear so quickly?

"Do you have a credit card?" Kane asked, surprising her again.

"Yes, I have one." Only one, for emergencies. She tried to pay cash for everything.

"Good. When you need to spend money on a client, charge it on your card and write an expense report. We'll reimburse you the amount before your credit card bill comes in."

"I—I see."

"Good. The other problem is you taking Jack out alone. Do you have a—" He broke off and frowned. "Hell, I should've asked Maggie to do this."

"Do what?" She thought she was in real trouble this time.

"Well, I'm just going to ask. Do you have a boyfriend?"

Now Sharon was thoroughly confused. "No, sir."

He stared at her as if she were an oddity. "Well, okay, then Andy or I will accompany you a time or two, to give you some support."

"Yes, sir," she said, relieved that her problem was being solved.

"Good. It's not a question of your competence, you understand. Just—propriety. Protecting ourselves and Jack of any possible misunderstanding." He sighed with relief and leaned back in his chair. "Do you have any questions?"

"No, sir."

"Jack was very complimentary about your work so far. You're making me look good, and I like that," Kane added, smiling. "Even if Jack doesn't drop any more hints, an occasional dinner or tickets to something he'd like to see is a good idea. Keep the client happy."

"Yes, sir."

"There's not anything between you two already, is there? I'm picking up on something."

Okay, so she wasn't out of the woods, yet. But she'd already told Andy, so she might as well tell Kane, too. "Actually, sir, there is one little thing."

"Yes?" Kane leaned forward, frowning.

"Jack is the man I was trapped in the elevator with."

"What?" Kane roared with horror, leaping to his feet. "Why didn't I know that? Good Lord, it's a wonder he ever signed with us. Maggie!"

Sharon didn't move, not sure what she should do.

Maggie came rushing in. "Kane, what's wrong? Everyone in the building will hear you."

"Jack was the man in the elevator with Sharon. He must think we're indifferent to his suffering. Get him on the phone and set up a nice dinner this evening. At a very expensive restaurant. Sharon and I and Andy, yes, call Andy and tell him when and where to meet us. We're taking Jack to dinner this evening. And tell Jack to bring a lady friend if he'd like. Whatever he wants!"

"Yes, sir," Maggie agreed briskly, making notes on a pad in her hand. "Would Le Cirque be appropriate?"

"Perfect! Thanks, Maggie," he said. "In fact, you come, too. You're good at social situations. That's not a problem, is it? You can come?"

"I can, Kane, but I'm sure you don't need me." Maggie was already backing out the door, obviously hoping to escape, or anxious to start calling.

"I need you. I'll pick you up at whatever time you say so you'll have time to go home and change. Leave when you have to."

Maggie rolled her eyes at Sharon and left the office.

"You're available tonight, aren't you?" He seemed to take her agreement for granted. "You can leave early, too. Take a cab to the restaurant and put it on your expense report.''

He was pacing the room and Sharon watched him in fascination. She'd known Kane was bright, kind, hard-working. But she'd never seen him like this.

''The time in the elevator, was he shaken up by it? Did it upset him, make him angry?''

Sharon managed a smile. ''No, he was quite calm and—and tried to soothe me. He was—was quite the gentleman.''

''Good. Of course. I guess that's why he seems more familiar with you. You two were trapped for quite a while. I had the elevators checked immediately. They're perfectly safe now,'' he assured her.

''Yes, that's what Maggie said.''

His door opened and Maggie entered, saying, ''I have a reservation for five at Le Cirque. Jack will be there but without a date. Andy agreed, too. You'll need to pick me up at seven as the earliest I could get a table was seven-thirty.''

''We could've gone later,'' Kane said, frowning.

''You maybe could, but I need my beauty sleep,'' she said stiffly and left the room.

Kane grinned. ''She's a pip, isn't she? Like she needs to be more beautiful, even if she tries hard to hide it.'' He chuckled to himself, as if unaware Sharon was his audience. Then he focused on her. ''Okay, so everything's arranged. If you need directions to the restaurant, ask Maggie. We'll see you there at seven-thirty. Oh, and the restaurant is French.''

''Thank you, sir.'' Sharon hurried from his office,

not bothering to tell him she'd had high-school French and three years at college. She loved the language even if she seldom had an opportunity to use it.

No, her problem wasn't French. It was more common to women worldwide.

"Maggie, what do I wear?"

"No little black dress?" Maggie asked, smiling sympathetically.

Sharon shook her head no. Her life had been class, studying and family. Nothing that required dress-up other than church.

"Okay, go to Filene's Basement. It's nearby and they have the best selection and prices. Get a simple black dress that you can change by wearing different accessories. It will come in handy now that you're management," She added with a grin.

"But I don't have time."

"Sure you do. Go pack up and leave. Kane gave you permission. Explain to Andy. It won't be a problem."

Maggie's soothing calm helped Sharon gain control. Good thing she had that charge card for emergencies. "You're sure?"

"I'm sure. Remember Mr. Waterton is an important client. By the way, why didn't you tell me he was the one in the elevator?"

"I didn't know until I met him in Kane's office the other day. I only knew the name Jack."

Maggie's eyes rounded in surprise. "That must've been a shock," she murmured.

"You can say that again," Sharon said with a sigh and hurried out of the office.

Jack got to the restaurant early. He was embarrassed about the invitation. He'd been teasing Sharon, hoping to have a meal with her, just the two of them, when Kane came along and thought he was hinting for freebies. Not that Kane couldn't afford to show him some hospitality since he would make a considerable amount on this particular job.

So he'd accepted the basketball tickets and dinner invitation. But the sudden invitation to Le Cirque, one of the most popular and expensive restaurants in Chicago? Tonight? He didn't understand what was going on.

Rather than entering the restaurant, waiting in the lobby with crowds of other people, he decided to stand outside in the night air and watch for Sharon's arrival.

Would she wear a suit? He hungered to see her in something feminine. Could he manage to sit by her tonight? Or would the two guard dogs, Andy and Kane, surround her?

He would just like a little personal conversation with her. Like asking her if her father was in construction. And if she had any boyfriends. If she was involved with anyone. Did his making love to her cause her any problems?

He should've contacted her at once. He knew that, but the timing had been off. What if her boyfriend had dumped her because she'd been intimate with him? Then he'd owe her, big-time. He could offer to escort her when she needed one.

With a laugh at his self-sacrifice, he turned to see Maggie and Kane getting out of a sleek black Jaguar. Maggie was an attractive woman. Jack was glad his secretary was sixty years old and motherly. No temptation there.

"Evening, Jack. Wouldn't they seat you?" Kane asked, frowning as he handed his keys to the parking attendant.

"I didn't ask. I thought I'd enjoy the fresh air for a few minutes. It's crowded in there."

"Come with us. We'll have them seat us at once and get out of the crowd," Kane insisted as he led the way, his hand guiding Maggie in front of him.

In no time, they were seated at one of the prime tables, on a raised tier of the floor to one side. Jack knew it took a lot of pull to get one of these tables on short notice. His estimation of Kane went up several inches.

"Nice job, Maggie. I'll never know how you do it," Kane said, destroying Jack's admiration for him. "Will they be able to get Andy's chair up here?"

Jack had forgotten about that complication.

"Yes. There's a ramp the waiters use. They promised it wouldn't be a problem."

Kane lifted her hand and kissed her knuckles. "You always think of everything." Maggie seemed discomfited by his behavior.

Jack had a few questions for Kane after his careful discussion earlier today. But Andy's arrival distracted him.

Which left only Sharon.

Jack kept his eyes glued to the front of the restaurant, eager for her to appear. Only when Kane began to explain the reason for their dinner did he look at him.

"Sharon told us you were the one trapped in the elevator with her," Kane said, apology lacing his words. "I can't believe I didn't discover that until today. Why didn't you tell me?"

"I was glad it was kept secret." And he wished it still was. What exactly had Sharon said? Surely she hadn't told them he'd made love to her.

"She told me you were—" Kane began and then broke off, standing. "Good evening, Sharon. Glad you could make it," he said with a smile.

Jack turned at once and stared at the woman in front of him. Sharon's hair was swept up in a complicated twist, reminding him more of her appearance in the elevator, when her hair had been pulled back. She wore delicate gold earrings, but no other jewelry, and a lace shawl that complemented the black simplicity of her dress, a formfitting sheath with a V-neck that hinted at what was beneath.

He took a deep breath. There was no boxy jacket to hide her figure tonight. If she'd been dressed like this on the job this morning, he wouldn't have gotten any work out of his men all day long.

He rose to pull out the chair next to him, grateful it had been left for her. Andy would be on her other side. "You look lovely, Sharon."

Her lashes swept down and her cheeks pinkened.

With a murmured thank you, she sat down in the chair. "I hope I'm not late. The cabbie got lost."

"But you'd gotten directions from Maggie, hadn't you?" Kane asked.

"Yes, thanks to your suggestion. He soon got back on track."

Jack noticed Maggie smiling at Sharon, then nodding, as if answering a question. He frowned and turned back to Sharon. "Everything all right?"

"Yes, of course." Her smile dimmed, but it was still a smile.

The waiter appeared and Kane ordered an expensive wine to start them off, but Maggie hurriedly said, "None for me, please."

"Me, neither," Sharon added, meeting Maggie's questioning look.

"Well, then, gentlemen, it looks like it'll be up to us he-men to drink the wine. But I think we'll be up to the challenge. Now, do we want appetizers?"

Before anyone could comment, he ordered a tray of various appetizers, then sent the waiter away until everyone could have time to study the menu.

He leaned over and whispered something to Maggie, but she shook her head no. Jack wished he could be as informal with Sharon. He had several things he'd like to whisper in her ear. But he also still had to worry about what she'd told Kane about being trapped in the elevator.

There was still a nibbling of suspicion that she might be trying to force him to offer marriage, or at least a money settlement, for what had happened. Not that she didn't deserve some recompense for his losing control, but he'd hate to discover that was her plan.

"As I was saying," Kane began again. "I had no idea you were the man trapped in the elevator. Sharon said you were a complete gentleman, of course, but I thought maybe dinner tonight would let you know how sorry we are that it happened."

The alluring woman beside him didn't raise her gaze from the menu.

"Thanks, Sharon, for praising me. I thought, between the two of us, we got through it pretty well."

"Sharon had to have stitches," Maggie said. "Did you suffer a like fate, Jack?"

"No, I didn't. I'm not sure where Sharon cut herself, either. You haven't told me what happened, Sharon."

She looked at him as if he'd made a big mistake. Then she muttered, "The cut was nothing. We're fortunate there were no bigger injuries. And I really appreciate that you had the elevators checked at once, Kane."

Jack didn't repeat that question. But he made a mental note to ask it again, when they were alone.

Andy reached over and turned Sharon's arm. "Is it going to leave a scar?" he asked.

Sharon pulled her arm away. "I'm sure it won't."

"We can pay for plastic surgery," Kane offered.

"No, please, I'm fine. I saw the blueprints of Jack's project this morning. It's going to be a magnificent building." Sharon obviously didn't want to be in the limelight.

Jack assisted her by telling several amusing stories

about the project coming together. All the while, he went over the cut, the praise she'd heaped upon him without revealing what had actually occurred. Was she setting him up for blackmail?

The picture she presented made that hard to believe, but he'd been around for a while. His wife had had a butter-wouldn't-melt-in-my-mouth look, but she'd trapped him into marriage.

But being trapped by Sharon wouldn't be all bad. He'd have the right to touch her, then. To hold her against him all through the night. To make his dreams real. Maybe then he'd get a decent night's sleep. Or at least losing his sleep would be for a worthwhile purpose.

He realized the waiter had returned and the two ladies were ordering. Both did so in flawless French. He stared at Sharon in surprise. "Good job. Willing to help me? I was never good at languages."

"Of course. Do you know what you want?" She blushed and added, "I mean, steak, chicken, fish?"

"Steak," he said firmly.

She told him his choices, then reminded him that the French served steak rare. He ordered his medium-well. The waiter wrote his order down with a sneer of disdain on his face. Since Andy and Kane also wanted their steaks cooked, Jack didn't feel bad.

When the waiter had left the table, Maggie told a story about traveling in France. When she'd finished, Jack asked Sharon if she'd traveled in France, since her accent was so good.

"No, but I had some excellent teachers."

Kane leaned forward. "Don't you want to go?"

"Yes, I do, but I just finished my degree, Kane, and I hope to get my Master's also. Someday I'll manage to go," she assured him with a calm smile.

Immediately, Jack envisioned himself showing the beauty of Paris to Sharon. He knew, from her interest today that she'd love the architecture. "Do you like art?"

"Most art. I'm a fan of the Impressionists."

"Then you definitely must go to Paris."

She nodded. "But I'm not deprived of art here in Chicago. We have great museums. I go to the Art Institute frequently, and there are a lot of smaller museums."

"Too bad you couldn't go with that lady yesterday. What was her name?"

Jack realized Kane was watching them and wasn't surprised when Kane questioned Sharon. She explained, "Deedee West was in our department. She had a spare ticket for a showing at the Art Institute."

Andy snapped his fingers. "Oh, that's the showing of the armor through the ages. It's amazing how small men were back then. Neither of you guys could fit into any of it."

Sharon was surprised that she enjoyed herself. The food was delicious. She was glad she'd chosen chicken, along with Maggie. The steaks were cooked medium, at best, and she couldn't have faced it.

Her dress had been a surprise, too. She had found it almost at once, and it had fitted perfectly. And, as Maggie had said, the price was reasonable. She'd already thought of several different ways to change it.

She'd borrowed her mother's shawl tonight, a long-ago gift from an elderly aunt.

In fact, everything had gone well. Maybe she could do this after all. As long as she had someone with her. In addition to the man beside her. Just sitting next to him brought back so many memories of their time in the elevator. A time she needed to forget.

She switched her thoughts to her mother. Tonight, she and her beau had gone out to dinner, too. He seemed very nice. Her mother had met him at church, and they'd become friends first. But Sharon couldn't help but worry. It would destroy her mother if she were betrayed again.

She suddenly realized everyone was getting ready to leave. "Oh, sorry, I was daydreaming," she said with a smile and stood to gather her shawl around her.

"We couldn't convince you two ladies to have dessert, so I guess we'll have to end the evening," Kane said with a teasing look. "Besides, Maggie says she needs her beauty sleep."

Jack said, "I can't imagine any two women who are in less need of more beauty."

"Nicely said," Maggie returned with a smile.

Sharon felt much more awkward. "Thank you," she murmured.

Suddenly, she remembered she needed to call a taxi. She'd get the concierge to do so when they got to the front of the restaurant.

When they reached the lobby, it was as crowded as when they came in. But she stepped to the podium and asked the gentleman to call a cab.

"Not necessary," Jack said and handed several bills to the man.

"What are you doing? I need to get home."

He took her elbow and moved her toward the door. "I'll see you home. I'm not sure it's safe to take a cab alone this late in the evening."

There was one cab standing outside the restaurant and Sharon tried to head toward it, but Andy rolled to it before she managed more than a step. She knew Andy lived in the opposite direction to her, so she didn't arm wrestle Jack for her freedom.

Kane turned around, after giving his receipt to the parking attendant. "Oh, Sharon! I forgot about getting you a cab. Let me—"

"I'm taking her home," Jack said firmly.

Kane stared at him, but Sharon noted that Jack's gaze flicked to Maggie, then back to Kane.

"All right with you, Kane?" he asked.

Something was going on. Sharon just wasn't sure what.

"Yes, thank you, Jack. I'm sure Sharon will appreciate the ride. It's a nice, friendly gesture."

"Yeah. Thanks for the dinner. It was a pleasure."

"We enjoyed it, too. See you tomorrow, Sharon."

Maggie bid her goodbye, too. And Sharon was left standing on the sidewalk, in Jack's clutches.

Chapter Seven

Jack laughed at himself under his breath. He felt like a middle-school boy, dying to get the girl alone, but not sure what to do once he does.

He looked at Sharon. "Comfy?"

"Sure. Who wouldn't be in this car?" she asked, rubbing her hand on the leather seat. "Very nice."

"Thanks." He was proud of his car, a Mercedes. "Better than a taxi?"

She shot him a look that told him he was pushing. "You know it is, but there was no need for you to take me home. I would've been fine in a taxi."

"I know, but I don't ever get you alone."

She did a double take. "Don't be ridiculous. We don't need to be alone."

"Yes, we do. I have lots I want to ask you."

She seemed to shrink within herself, which worried him. Was she hiding something? What did she fear he might ask her?

"Like, was your father in construction? You were so relaxed with my crew, I thought—"

"My father, for the five years I knew him, sold insurance." Her voice was clipped. No regret in it.

"Five years?"

"I told you in the elevator he wasn't in the picture."

"Yeah, but I didn't realize he—you were only five. Did he die?"

"Nope. He just moved on to greener fields, leaving my mother with five children. I'm the oldest."

He noticed she was staring out the passenger window, not looking at him. "That must've been hard."

"We managed."

"And that's why you still live at home, helping your brothers and sisters get through school?"

"Someone had to."

He chuckled again.

"What?" she demanded, irritation in her voice.

"I was thinking about what my sister's response would be. The least selfish thing she does is shop."

Sharon stared at him. "Why is that unselfish?"

"Because she's doing her part to fuel the economy," he explained, mock surprise on his face.

Sharon couldn't hold back a chuckle. "That's an interesting theory."

He liked making her laugh. Even in the elevator, he'd distracted her from her fears long enough to occasionally hear that sexy laugh of hers.

"I gather your sister doesn't have money shortages?"

"None of my family does. Didn't you know?"

A bewildered look on her face encouraged him.

"No. I know Kane said you're an important client but—I assumed your company was doing okay."

"It's doing more than okay, but I didn't work my way up from poverty."

"Lucky you."

"Could be lucky you if you intend to sue me." He purposely didn't look at her, keeping his gaze on the road.

Sharon said nothing for several minutes, and Jack figured he'd surprised her by guessing her intent.

"Is that what is going on? You wanted to talk to me because you're afraid I'll sue you?" she asked, her words stiff. "You think I'll sue you for having sex with me in the elevator?"

"I lost control. You may think I owe you for that."

"You lost control because I lost control first. If I hadn't had hysterics, I doubt we would've progressed as we did."

He risked a glance out of the corner of his eye and found her staring straight ahead, her jaw squared.

"So, you're not going to sue me?"

"No. Do you want me to sign a release? Have your lawyer draw something up. I'll sign it and fax it to you. You won't have to waste any more time on our 'incident'."

She crossed her arms across her chest and looked away.

"That wasn't the only reason I wanted to spend time with you, honey," he murmured gently.

"My name is Sharon, not honey," she snapped.

He tried to make amends for her anger. "What we shared was special, Sharon, but I had to know—"

"That the price wasn't too high? So you see me as a high-priced prostitute? I suppose I should be pleased that you don't think I'm a common, run-of-the-mill lady of the evening."

"Stop that! I'm trying to tell you—"

"I don't want to hear anything you have to tell me. Just stay away from me." She turned her shoulders away and leaned her head against the window.

"Sharon, you've misunderstood."

Nothing.

Okay, fine, he'd let her sulk for a while. She'd given him directions to her home earlier. They drove in silence. Occasionally, he'd look in her direction for some letup in animosity, but she remained turned away.

Coming to a stop in front of her house, he put the car in park and turned off the engine. Still she didn't move. "Do you want to have a civil discussion now?" he finally asked.

She refused to answer him, which only irritated him more. Definitely being difficult. He reached out and touched her arm. "Sharon?"

A slight sound startled him. He leaned forward so he could see her face, and the noise was repeated. A ladylike snore. Sharon had fallen asleep.

He couldn't believe it. He'd waited for her to get over her snit, to apologize for exaggerating. Instead of agonizing over their conversation, she fell asleep.

He shook her arm. "Sharon?"

Her head lolled back against the soft leather, but

If offer card is missing write to: Silhouette Reader Service, 3010 Walden Ave., P.O. Box 1867, Buffalo NY 14240-1867

NO POSTAGE
NECESSARY
IF MAILED
IN THE
UNITED STATES

BUSINESS REPLY MAIL
FIRST-CLASS MAIL   PERMIT NO. 717-003   BUFFALO, NY

POSTAGE WILL BE PAID BY ADDRESSEE

SILHOUETTE READER SERVICE
3010 WALDEN AVE
PO BOX 1867
BUFFALO NY 14240-9952

Play The *Lucky Hearts* Game

and get...
FREE BOOKS & a FREE GIFT... YOURS to KEEP!

Scratch Here!
then look below to see
what your cards get you...

Yes! I have scratched off the silver card.
Please send me my **2 FREE BOOKS**
and **FREE MYSTERY GIFT**. I understand
that I am under no obligation to purchase any
books as explained on the back of this card.

315 SDL DC55   **215 SDL DC5Y**

NAME   (PLEASE PRINT CLEARLY)

ADDRESS

APT.#   CITY

STATE / PROV.   ZIP/POSTAL CODE

Twenty-one gets you
2 FREE BOOKS and a
FREE MYSTERY GIFT!

Twenty gets you
2 FREE BOOKS!

Nineteen gets you
1 FREE BOOK!

TRY AGAIN!

Offer limited to one per household and not valid to current
Silhouette Romance® subscribers. All orders subject to approval.

Visit us online at
www.eHarlequin.com

she didn't awaken. He stared at her. What was he supposed to do now? Unlocking his door, he circled the car and opened hers, practically catching her as she fell into his arms.

Lifting her against his chest, he pushed the door shut with his shoe. "Baby, when you sleep, you really sleep," he muttered. He'd never seen anyone sleep so deeply.

He crossed the modest lawn and hoped her mother was home to open the door. Leaning on the doorbell with his elbow, he then stood back and waited.

The door swung open and an attractive woman, quite similar to Sharon in looks, stared at him, surprise on her face, then concern. "Sharon! Is she all right?"

"She's asleep. I tried to wake her, but she must be really tired."

Her mother hesitated, then said, "She sleeps deeply," she assured him as she swung open the door. "Do you mind carrying her to her bedroom?"

"Of course not." In fact, he kind of liked carrying her. Besides, it was a one-story house.

A man appeared behind the woman. "Is everything all right, Edith?"

"Yes. Sharon has fallen asleep," she said to him with a soft smile that told Jack a lot.

"Right down the hall, the first door on the left," Edith called out as Jack moved past her.

He nudged open the door, stopping a minute to stare at Sharon's personal space. There was no coldness here. Memories filled the room, from pictures to keepsakes. There were twin beds, very fiftyish. It was tidier than he would've expected, but most of all, it was warm and welcoming.

Hearing a step behind him, he asked, "Which bed?"

"The one by the window," Edith said. "Let me turn down the covers first."

She did so, and he eased Sharon to the bed, reluctantly withdrawing his arms. Without ever opening her eyes, Sharon turned on her side and curled into her pillow.

He frowned. She must need the sleep badly.

Edith said softly, "I appreciate your carrying her in, Mr. Waterton."

"You know who I am?" he asked in surprise.

"She told me she was going to dinner with you, Andy and Mr. Haley. I've met both of them so I assumed—"

"Right. Look, I'll call Kane in the morning and let him know, but I don't want you to wake Sharon in the morning. Let her sleep in. I'm worried about her health."

Edith stared at him, surprise on her face. "You are?"

"This kind of exhaustion isn't normal."

"Oh, but—yes, you're probably right. Thank you for your concern. You're sure it will be all right for her to go in late?"

"Oh, yeah. Tell her I'll talk to her tomorrow afternoon." Then he wrenched his gaze away from the beautiful young woman who seemed to occupy his mind most of the time. "Good night," he said and left the house.

* * *

Sharon stretched beneath the covers, a smile on her lips. She felt good. She didn't often sleep in on Saturday mornings, but she was glad she hadn't set her alarm.

After last night's—last night was Thursday. Today wasn't Saturday. It was Friday. Her eyes snapped open to stare at the alarm clock beside her bed. It was ten-fifteen.

When she finally took in the time, she sat bolt upright. Ten-fifteen! She couldn't imagine what had happened. Last night she'd gone to dinner with Kane, Maggie and Andy…and Jack. Then Jack had insisted on taking her home.

After he'd accused her of intending to sue him, her memory stopped. Oh, dear, she'd fallen asleep.

But how had she gotten into bed?

She got up and began racing about the room, gathering her clothes, until her head and stomach told her to stop. She sank back down, taking deep breaths to control the nausea. Remain calm.

As she followed her own advice, she saw the note.

Dear Sharon,
Mr. Waterton said for you to sleep in. He would explain to your boss. Hope that's okay. You certainly seemed to need to sleep.

Love Mom

Sharon lost her focus on staying calm, wishing Jack was close enough for her to kick him in the shins.

What was he trying to do, ruin her career as well as her life?

She grabbed the phone and dialed Andy's number.

When he answered, she began in a rush. "Andy, it's Sharon. I overslept. I'll be in by noon and will work late this evening to make up for it. I'm so sorry."

"I already know, Sharon. Are you all right?"

"Of course I am! What did that idiot tell you? That I had sleeping sickness? I can't believe he convinced my mother to follow his direction. It won't happen again, I promise you, Andy."

"Kane wants you to get checked out. When you come in, you can set up an appointment."

Sharon didn't argue the point now. But she would. First she had another phone call to make. She dialed again.

"Mr. Waterton's office," a sweet voice said.

With her teeth gritted together, Sharon, said, "Is he in?"

"May I ask who's calling?"

"Sharon."

"Oh, just a minute, please."

Like he'd left instructions to always put her through. She didn't think so.

"Sharon? How are you this morning."

"Not so good since I'm missing half a day's work, thanks to you. How dare you interfere in my business!"

"I thought you needed the rest." His voice was calm with just a tinge of amusement that drove her crazy.

Spacing her words for emphasis, she said, "Don't you ever make decisions for me again!" Then she hung up.

She hoped she never saw the man again! Not that he'd seek her out, now that she'd assured him she had no intention of suing him. That had been his only concern. She headed for the kitchen and a glass of milk before she got ready for work. And maybe a scrambled egg or two. She needed her strength.

When she showed up for work at noon, Alice was at her desk. "How are you, dear? Were you sick again this morning?"

"No, Alice, I wasn't." She tried to keep her voice calm. After all, it wasn't Alice's fault she was late. "Someone decided I should sleep in and turned off my alarm."

"Maybe it was for the best," Alice said, still smiling.

"It won't be for the best if I lose my job. They had no right to—never mind. I'm here now and I'll get my work done."

"Of course you will. Here are your messages." With a coy smile, she said, "That nice Mr. Waterton has called several times."

Sharon clenched her teeth and said nothing. That nice Mr. Waterton could call as much as he wanted, but she wasn't going to return his calls.

The one from Pete, Jack's field manager, caught her eye. She hurriedly dialed his number.

"Pete, this is Sharon. Is there a problem?"

"Well, sort of. I can't get hold of Jack and a vendor

has a question about two statements he's got. I just thought you could give us an answer.''

"Is he still there?"

"Yeah, he is. Can you come over now?"

"I'll be right there."

"Thanks, Sharon."

She sighed. Another ride on the elevator. She turned to Alice. "I'm going to the job site, Alice."

"Of course."

She grabbed her briefcase so she'd have a calculator and pen and paper and headed back to the elevators.

When she crossed the street, she made her first stop at the temporary office to find her hard hat hanging on a nearby nail. She stuck it on her head and walked outside to meet Pete with a big barrel-chested man in his late fifties.

She stuck out her hand and introduced herself.

"I'm Bill Waggoner. Glad to meet you."

"You have a question about a billing practice? On this job?"

"No, not this one, but this just came in the mail today, and I thought maybe Pete here could tell me what's going on, so I brought it with me." He handed Sharon two pieces of paper, both copies of an order.

"These here components are expensive pieces of machinery for the elevators."

She inwardly groaned. She couldn't seem to get away from those things. "Yes?"

"Well, this other job has four elevators, so they ordered ten, which was a lot, but hey, it's Jack's money. But when I got the copy of the order and the check for payment, there was another copy in the envelope for twenty of 'em.''

"Twenty?"

"Yeah, and he didn't order no twenty. And it shows my signature and Jack's on it."

So here was Jack's proof. A stupid clerical error, including the fake billing slip with the correct one to the vendor. "I see. I'm pretty sure I understand the problem, Mr. Waggoner, and it won't be a problem for you. May I keep this for a day or two?"

"Sure, I don't need it. Almost threw it out, thinking they must've made a mistake."

"I'm glad you didn't, and I'm sure Mr. Waterton will be glad also. Thank you. I'll return the real receipt in a few days and I'll let you know what happens," she promised. Then she nodded her thanks to Pete and crossed the street again, after dropping off her hard hat.

Now she had to return Jack's call, because she was pretty sure she had evidence that his accountant was scamming him for money.

When she entered her department, she discovered she was wrong. She didn't have to call Jack. He was sitting at her desk, waiting for her.

"Good afternoon," she said stiffly.

He stood, smiling, as if nothing personal had ever been spoken between them. Maybe she should sue him just to upset him.

"Would you join me in the conference room?" she suggested firmly enough to let him know it was an order. Then she spun on her heels and crossed the hall to the private area.

"Testy today, aren't we?" he asked with an even bigger grin.

She closed her eyes and counted to ten. It didn't help that much, but at least she should get credit for trying.

"One of your vendors had a question."

"Which one?" he asked, snapping to business mode at once.

"Bill Waggoner. He asked Pete, who asked me." She slapped the two copies on the table. "Take a look." She sat down to await his response.

After looking at both papers, he fell into a chair beside her. "Here's my proof." He wasn't exultant. If anything, he sounded depressed.

"I'd hoped I was wrong," he finally added. "We've been friends for a long time. I should've pursued it more vigorously, but I kept thinking he'd stop."

"That rarely happens," she said softly, not wanting to sympathize with him, but she knew a friend's betrayal hurt.

"I'm going to have to get him out of there and have a complete accounting done. Can you take it on?"

"Not and do my job properly. However, we have an excellent forensic accounting department. They'll be able to straighten it out and give you a proper accounting of the damage done. Shall I call them?"

With a heavy sigh, he agreed.

She picked up the conference-room phone and called the proper office. In no time, several men joined them in the conference room. Sharon briefly explained the situation and then let Jack take over.

As she excused herself, he said, "Oh, and, honey, can you call my office and tell my secretary I'll be out the rest of the day? Thanks."

The two accountants sent speculative glances her way, and she fought to keep the red from her cheeks. She was going to kill him. Calling her honey in front of them made their relationship appear a lot more than professional.

"Certainly, *Mr. Waterton!*" Then she flounced out of the room.

As soon as she sat down at her desk and took a deep breath, she picked up the phone and dialed Jack's office.

"This is Sharon from Kane Haley, Inc. Mr. Waterton asked me to call and tell you he'd be out of the office the rest of the day."

The sweet voice from earlier said, "Oh, dear. And I don't suppose he has his cell phone on, does he?"

"I don't know. Is there a problem?"

"Roger has been trying to call him. Said he has a question that only Jack can answer. He's always so full of himself!" the lady complained.

"Mr. Waterton is still here. Shall I ask him to call you?"

"Could you, please? That would be such a help."

"I'll do so right away."

She didn't want to go back into the conference room, but she had no choice. She crossed the hall and knocked on the now-closed door. Then she stuck her head inside.

"Mr. Waterton, your secretary asked that you call her right away. Roger has been calling with a question that he won't reveal to her."

"Thanks, Sharon, and wait a second, will you?"

Like she had a choice now. She stood there while he talked briefly with his secretary. Then he dialed another number. "Roger? What's up? Libby said you'd been calling.

"Well, that sounds like a good deal, but let's wait a day or two. I don't want to get overextended just to have a few backups.

"Uh-uh. I think you exceeded your authority, Roger. Call them back and withdraw the order." He paused, his look intense. "I'll drop by in a few minutes to talk about this."

Finally he ended the conversation.

Then he turned to Sharon. "Call Kane and tell him I'm going to need your company to take over my other two projects at once."

She felt like saluting, as if she were a private and he was the general. But there was that heartsickness in his eyes that touched her. So she stuffed her resentment away and nodded. Then she closed the door behind her.

Chapter Eight

Jack normally enjoyed his work. He liked building something, knowing that when he finished his job, there would be a building that people could use, enjoy.

But today had been a day that made him want to withdraw from the world. Today, he'd lost a friend.

He and Roger Mallick had met just before Jack had decided to go out on his own. He'd invited Roger to become a partner in the business. Roger had refused, not willing to put his own money into the firm, but he'd agreed to be the head of accounting. Well, then, it had been the entire accounting department.

After five years, Jack had again offered Roger the opportunity to become part-owner. He'd felt bad that he was doing so well and Roger, though he received a good salary, wasn't getting to share in the profits. But he'd refused.

When Jack was married, the two couples had done a lot together. Roger had children and Jack was their godfather. Their lives were intertwined. And, according to the accountants who'd gone with him to Roger's office, he'd been stealing from Jack in increasing amounts for the past five years.

When he'd confronted Roger, the man hadn't apologized. He'd told Jack he deserved the money. He didn't believe he'd done anything wrong. The accountants suggested he have Roger arrested. Jack didn't know if he could do that. He'd had the locks changed, his account at the bank closed and a new one opened. Roger's name had been removed from any access to his company.

He got off the elevator. He couldn't explain what he was doing here, either. Telling himself he wanted to be sure Sharon had lined up more accountants to take over in the morning, he'd driven to Kane Haley, Inc. It was almost six o'clock, but he was hoping Sharon was still here. He'd called her home and her mother had said she was going to work late.

It was Friday night. The office was empty when he stepped into the Special Projects area, except for one beautiful woman. She sat at her desk, her head down, working.

"Sharon?"

She jumped, her face reflecting her surprise. One hand went to her throat. "You—you startled me," she exclaimed. Taking a deep breath, she leaned back in her chair. "What do you need, Jack?"

"Did you talk to Kane?"

"Yes, of course. Did—did everything go all right?"

"I guess." How could it be all right when a man you trusted stabbed you in the back and didn't care?

"Kane said to tell you he's sorry, but we'll do everything we can to help you through this."

He stared at those light green eyes of hers, seeing sympathy in them. He'd known he wouldn't get any sympathy from his family. Oh, they would rant and rave about the lost money, but not about the lost friend. They wouldn't understand.

Somehow he'd known that Sharon would.

"It was awful," he muttered, frowning fiercely.

He heard her move, but he didn't look up. Then she touched his arm.

"I imagine it must've been. Did he express remorse?"

"No, none. All this time I thought he was a good friend. I trusted him!" His voice was growing louder, closer to losing control and he gasped for air.

She said nothing and he looked up. Her eyes were glistening with tears, much to his surprise. "Jack, I'm a friend now, not your accountant, okay?"

He didn't understand what she was saying until her arms slid around him and she laid her head against his chest. "I'm so sorry," she whispered. "I know that must've hurt."

He clutched her to him. How had she known? Her heat began to warm and fill the hollow spot inside him that ached. He stood there, holding her against him for the longest time, until another kind of feeling began to assert itself. As it had on the elevator.

She was so sweet, no wonder making love to her had been incredible. But he wouldn't let himself get out of control again.

He stepped back. "Thank you. I'm a little old to ask for a hug, but it helped."

"You're welcome." She moved back toward her desk, but he took her arm to stop her. "Yes?"

"I want you to come to dinner with me," he said, his voice gruff, prepared for her refusal.

She stared at him, and he saw a debate in her eyes and held his breath.

"Okay, as long as it's somewhere simple. I couldn't take French cuisine two nights in a row." She smiled, as if she hadn't surprised him.

"You will?"

"Yes, I'm hungry." She pulled from his hold and began straightening her desk. Stacking folders, she opened her briefcase and placed them inside. Then she turned to him. "Ready? There's a diner a block away, near my El stop. Is that okay?"

He knew the one she meant. It was clean, the food simple but good. Tonight, it didn't matter where they ate. But he wanted company. Sharon's company. "Yeah, that'll be fine." Then he'd take her home.

Sharon knew she was breaking the rules Kane had established for her protection. But when she'd needed strong arms to hold her, to help her through the time in the elevator, Jack had been there for her.

When he'd come into the office, pain in his gaze, a hug had been the only thing she could give. And she had.

Now he needed company, someone who would understand his misery. Someone who would coax him to eat and listen to his agony. Someone who cared.

That was the scary part. She cared. Last night, she'd been angry with him for asking her if she was going to sue. Even the anger had been because she cared.

Pretenses and lies had been stripped away in that elevator, when she'd thought she was going to die. In Jack she'd found a basic attraction combined with a caring that meant a great deal. They'd connected.

Now that she knew more about him, more details that is, she cared for him even more. So she had to be careful. She had to keep her distance. She had to protect her heart.

But tonight, she had to be his friend.

When they'd settled in a booth across from each other, Jack tried to tell her how much he appreciated her presence.

She reached across the table to put both her soft hands on top of his clenched ones. "You were there for me when I needed you."

Pain shot through him. "So this is payback? Is that all it is?"

"No, this is someone caring, Jack."

His anger melted. His hands pulled from beneath hers only to catch them and hold them there. "Thank you. I didn't have anyone who would understand except you." Strange to say that. He had friends. A lot of friends. But he wasn't close with anyone. His parents had never taught him intimacy.

In the elevator, he'd had no choice. He'd reached

out to Sharon because her hysteria made it absolutely necessary. He'd been more intimate with Sharon, both emotionally and physically, than he'd ever been with anyone.

"You folks ready to order?" a tired waitress asked, standing ready with her pen and pad.

He didn't turn Sharon loose. "What's the special today?"

"Meatloaf plate. Comes with mashed potatoes, green beans, and apple pie for dessert," she rattled off.

"Okay, Sharon?"

She nodded.

"We'll both have the special. And coffee."

"I'll have water, no coffee," Sharon added.

"Got it," the woman said, and left them alone.

He was still holding her hands, loving their warmth, but he didn't know what to say.

Quietly, she said, "Tell me what happened."

Somehow, going through the events of the day made sense. It gave him a focus. At the end, he said, "The forensic accountants said there was more than enough evidence to convict him, that I should press charges."

"They're right."

"Sharon, I can't do that. Because he betrayed me doesn't mean I can put him in jail."

The waitress appeared with their meal and he was forced to release her hands. He sat back, frowning.

When the waitress had left, he picked up his fork, suddenly wanting to avoid conversation.

"Jack, he needs to pay a price for what he's done.

And you need to send a message to the next accountant you hire.''

"Yeah, but does his wife need to pay a price? And their kids?''

"Did you pay him a good salary?''

"Hell, yes!'' He named the salary he'd considered generous.

She looked impressed. "You're right. That was a generous salary.''

"I offered twice to make him a principle in the company, but he was never willing to invest any of his money.''

Sharon shook her head. "Why bother taking a risk when he could just steal it?'' she said, sarcasm filling her voice.

"Yeah.''

"That's why you have to press charges. For him to know he did something wrong. Let his children know he did something wrong. Let all of them know that society doesn't accept his behavior.''

"That's the thing that bothered me most. I began to think I was in the wrong,'' he finally said. "Not him.''

She stretched one hand across again and he caught it in his. "No, Jack, he's the one who's wrong. You've earned your way.''

"I didn't have to struggle like a lot of people.'' He'd always felt a little guilty for his wealthy background.

"Jack, your family wealth didn't make your company prosper. Your hard work did that.'' She squeezed his hand. "Eat your dinner.''

He automatically took a bite and suddenly found himself hungry. He'd waited in her office that afternoon to have lunch with Sharon, but she'd presented him with proof of Roger's traitorous behavior and suddenly food had seemed unimportant. Now he was hungry.

After several minutes of devouring his meal, he paused. "So you really think I should press charges?"

"Yes, I do. It won't be easy, but I think it's the right thing to do."

He cleaned his plate. "I don't suppose you want to go with me to talk to the police?"

"Tonight?"

"Yeah, if I don't go now, I won't go. It's too hard to think of his family. I can make it without the money he took, but—yeah, tonight."

She sighed and looked at her watch. "Sure, I can go with you after we finish our meal."

He frowned. "You got a heavy date tonight?" Her checking the time hadn't made him happy.

"I don't think that's any of your business," she said stiffly, squaring her shoulders.

"Oh, you're back to the accountant mode? No longer a friend?" He felt the loss deeply.

"I have to be careful. You called me honey in front of two of our accountants, Jack. Rumors will soon start flying."

"I did? When?"

"When you asked me to call your secretary." Her beautiful lips were pressed together.

"Damn. I didn't mean to. But I was upset. I'll be careful, I promise."

"It doesn't matter. As long as we don't spend time together outside of the company, I can always deny anything. And you could call the lady you met at my desk, Deedee West, and accept her invitation."

"Why would I do that?"

"Because it would create gossip about you and her to distract people. I don't think she'll turn down any invitation you offer."

"I don't think she will either, but why would I want to offer anything?"

"Isn't she your type?"

The waitress's arrival with their pie stopped him from answering immediately, a good thing. He'd almost told her she was his type. But he wasn't ready to commit to anything. Not yet. When the waitress had gone again, he said, "I don't have a type."

Sharon shrugged her shoulders and took a bite of pie. "Oh, this is good. I shouldn't eat it but—"

"Why not? You're not overweight. In fact, you look like you might've lost a little weight. Are you eating all right?"

She didn't look up. "Just fine, thank you."

Suddenly, after their intimate conversation, they had nothing to say to each other? He leaned forward. "Where did you go?"

She looked up, surprise on her face. "I'm still here."

"My friend isn't here. My accountant is."

"You're right. But that's the way it has to be. Especially when we go to the police department."

He sighed. "Okay. But I like the friend better."

"You'll come see Kane Monday morning about the new business?"

"Do I need to? He can't just send someone over to my office?"

"I think he assumed you'd come." She took the last bite of her pie and closed her eyes, savoring the taste.

Jack forgot the question, watching her.

"Will you?"

"Hmmm? Oh, yeah. I'll meet you for coffee in the cafeteria and then—"

"No. Monday mornings are pretty hectic. And I lost a lot of time today, so I can't take any time off on Monday."

"You're saying that because of the rumors, aren't you?" he asked, his temper rising again.

"Jack, I've already explained to Kane that we became—close in the elevator. But he expects me to maintain a professional relationship with you."

"What if he hears about tonight?"

"I'll tell him I convinced you to go to the police, and it only seemed fair to offer you my support."

Her quick reply irritated him. "You're mighty fast with the excuses."

She didn't respond. "Could you ask her for our ticket?" At the same time she reached for her purse.

"Don't even think about it."

Her head came up. "Think about what?"

"Paying for your meal."

"Why not? You're my client. I'm going to pay for yours, too."

"No, you're not. The lady who came in here with

me was my friend. She didn't stay long, but I'm paying for her meal and mine, too.''

After staring at him, she apparently realized it would be a useless battle. Shrugging, she nodded.

Once they left the diner, he put a hand on her back and guided her toward his car.

''Is it far to the nearest precinct?'' she asked.

''A few blocks. It won't take long,'' he added, remembering her checking her watch.

He opened the car door and waited for her to get in. ''I promise not to fall asleep this time,'' she muttered.

''I would hope not. It's only a little after seven,'' he pointed out. ''Are you going to a doctor? Kane said he'd suggest one.''

Sharon had escaped addressing that problem all afternoon because she'd been so busy. Then, when she'd talked to Kane, it had been about Jack's business and he'd been too involved to think of other things.

Now she had to respond. ''That's not necessary.''

''I think it is. You were exhausted last night.''

''Yes, I was. Tension does that to me. But I just visited my doctor recently.''

''What did she say?''

She swallowed and sat quietly while he entered the stream of traffic. Visions of a wreck if she actually told him brought a smile to her face. When he turned to look at her, she wiped it away.

''She said I—I have a female problem that's temporary, nothing to worry about.'' Most men avoided any talk about female problems. She was sure Jack would, too.

"What kind of female problem?" he asked.

"I don't want to talk about it. It's private."

"But—"

The persistent man! "No, Jack, I will not discuss it with you. I'm in no danger. If I get a little tired, I'll recover from it." In twenty years, maybe.

He found a parking place on the street across from the police precinct, and she marvelled at his luck.

"How do you always manage to do that?"

"What?"

"Always find a parking place. It's amazing."

He shrugged. "I'd say I'm lucky, but after today, it wouldn't sound convincing."

"At least the loss isn't going to destroy you. That should make you feel lucky," she pointed out. "If someone stole much from me, I'd be down for the count."

"And you're still not going to sue me? I told you I have money."

She stared at him, irritation filling her. "I guess you're talking to your accountant now, not your friend, right?"

"My friend so seldom appears, I guess you're right."

She got out of the car, suddenly not feeling so warm about the irritating man beside her.

Inside, they asked for the white-collar crimes division.

"Third floor, to the left after you get out of the

elevator,'' the desk sergeant said. ''Just a skeleton crew at night, though.''

''Thank you, officer,'' Jack said.

To Sharon's surprise, he grabbed her hand and headed in that direction.

''You don't have to force me. I said I'd go,'' she pointed out.

''Anytime elevators are involved, I'm afraid you'll quit on me.'' For some reason, he was grinning at her.

She didn't find that particular memory too amusing.

After a brief ride in the elevator, they found the department they needed. Two men were sitting at desks and they both looked up.

''Can we help you?''

''Yes, we'd like to report a crime,'' Jack said, still holding Sharon's hand.

Afraid it would make them look unprofessional, she tugged on her hand, but he held on tightly.

''If you were mugged, sir, you've come to the wrong department.''

''It's a white-collar crime. Right department?''

''Yes, sir. Come have a seat, you and the missus.'' The man stood and pulled two spare chairs over to his desk.

''I'm his accountant, not his wife,'' Sharon quickly said. Jack had dropped her hand after the man's comment, and she dug in her purse for a business card.

''Are you the guilty party?'' the detective asked, smiling.

''No! I—I thought I might be able to back up his

story,'' she said, appalled at how they'd handled the situation.

''My fault,'' Jack said. ''I was reluctant to charge the man with a crime, and she talked me into it.''

''She could talk me into a lot of stuff, too,'' the other detective said softly, staring at her.

Sharon was ready to let all three men have it as they grinned at each other.

Chapter Nine

Sharon spent most of the weekend trying to figure out what to do.

Jack had made the decision both easier and more difficult on Friday night. When he'd insisted on driving her home, she'd accepted gracefully. And she hadn't fallen asleep.

Which meant, when he parked in front of her home, she had to face him and say good-night.

"For this moment," he'd said with a charming smile, "We're friends, okay?"

She really hadn't figured out what was to come. So she'd seen no problem with agreeing. She'd nodded.

Without any more words, he'd swept her into his embrace, his lips covering hers. She was immediately transported to her last time in Jack's arms, when they'd carried the embrace to its ultimate conclusion. Hunger filled her. She wanted him to love her.

Only the memory of her job, her career, the one thing she'd dedicated her life to, made her pull away from him. She'd been proud of her strength—and devastated by her loss.

She'd told herself since she was five that men couldn't be trusted. Men couldn't be counted on. She'd stared at Jack, her heart pleading to trust him, her mind refusing.

"Sharon, I—this attraction is powerful."

"Yes," she'd whispered. She couldn't deny his words, not with her heart trying to jump out of her body.

"We're not in an elevator."

"No," she agreed, her voice shaking.

"But the feelings are still there. I think maybe we should explore it. Don't you?"

"How?"

"Spend time together."

"W-we can't."

"But, Sharon—"

She hadn't been able to calmly sit there and discuss the explosion that had occurred in her body when he kissed her. She'd opened the door and slid from his expensive car. Then she'd raced into her house and slammed the door behind her.

She'd stayed there listening until she'd heard his car drive away. Then she'd hurried to her room.

But she couldn't shut out her emotions, the longing that became a solid ache, the fears that made her tremble.

So the debate had begun. Did she resign as head

of the Waterton project—which could mean the loss of her promotion and her raise?

Or did she try to keep her distance, work as much with Pete as she could, rather than Jack? Refuse to be alone with him? Could she control herself? Or, an even greater question, could she control Jack?

On Sunday afternoon, her mother sat her down, trying to help her. When Sharon confessed her problem, Edith had tried to convince her daughter that some men could be trusted.

"Mother, he thought I was going to sue him. He didn't contact me after we got to the hospital. If we hadn't met by chance, I still wouldn't know the last name of my baby's father."

"True, those are points not in his favor. Have you discussed them with him?"

"He said he had some problems. He was out of town for a month and then got a big job and had a—a personal problem come up."

"But he intended to contact you?"

"When he got around to it. Maybe in five years or so. What difference does it make? I'm going to raise my baby alone. I don't need him...or his money."

But she wanted him. And that bothered her most of all.

Jack paced his condo most of the weekend.

He'd scared himself with his behavior Friday night. His need for Sharon was something he hadn't experienced before. He'd never needed his wife. He'd accommodated her movement into his life. He'd tolerated her lie, waited for the birth of his child. But he hadn't needed her.

He'd survived other disappointments alone. But Friday, he'd felt a real need for Sharon, for her touch, her understanding. Which made him vulnerable.

When he'd kissed her again, it had only taken the first touch for his body to go hard as a rock, for an aching need to take control of his mind. In the elevator, it had taken a while for him to reach the point of no return.

Friday night, he'd gone from zero to out-of-control in nothing flat. Only Sharon's reaction had stopped the stampede of emotions.

She didn't want him.

What now? Did he ask Kane to put someone else on his account? Would that reflect poorly on Sharon? He certainly didn't want to harm her, but he also didn't want to work with her. She would use it as an excuse.

He had no intentions of giving her up. No, a man didn't walk away from the feelings he'd been having. They were too rare, too powerful. So it would be better if he wasn't working with her. Then he could pursue her without complications.

Maybe he could explain to Kane.

He'd try that when he was there Monday morning.

Sharon wore red to work on Monday. For power.

"Nice suit," Alice assured her. "It looks really good with your hair. A real attention-getter."

"Thank you. I'm late because I went to the site across the street before I came up." She'd figured she'd kill two birds with one stone. Eliminate one elevator ride and take care of business with Pete before Jack got in the picture.

She'd definitely gotten the attention of the crew.

"Here are your calls," Alice said, handing her a stack of messages.

"Thanks." She shuffled through them. Yes, Jack had called. She sat down and called his office. Again, she was passed through at once.

"Morning, Sharon," his sexy voice said, and she almost melted. She questioned her decision. But she had to try.

"Jack, I've already talked to Pete this morning, so I think everything's on track."

"I was planning on visiting the site myself and checking a few things with you."

"I need to go over a few things with you, too. Can you meet me for a late breakfast in about half an hour at the diner we used Friday night?"

Silence followed her request, and she figured she'd surprised him. But she certainly couldn't have a discussion about their—about Friday night—here in the office. Or in front of his crew.

"Sure," he finally agreed, a smile in his voice. "I'd love to. I'll even pick up the tab. Half an hour? I'll be there."

So would she. But she'd pay the bill. In more ways than one.

She went to the copy room to duplicate some papers and ran into Lauren.

"Hi, Sharon. Are you coming to break today? We haven't seen you much lately."

"I know, and I miss talking to everyone, but I've been really busy lately. And I can't make it today, either. Tell everyone I said hi."

"Okay," Lauren agreed, shrugging her shoulders.

Sharon did miss the camaraderie she shared with the other women. And she liked to talk to Jen about her pregnancy, because she would be going through the same things. But not being able to tell anyone about it made asking questions difficult.

Her mother was being helpful. After four pregnancies, one a double bonus with the twins, she could answer most questions. There were minutes when Sharon considered telling everyone. After all, it wasn't a question of waiting for her to marry. She could imagine Jack's reaction when he heard. He'd figure it to be another trick to ensnare him into a marriage he didn't want.

The way his first wife had done.

When he'd told her that story in the elevator, as he'd held her, she'd been enraged for him. She still was. And she didn't want to be lumped into the same category.

Telling everyone about her pregnancy was an impossibility as long as Jack was around. And she wanted him to remain in the picture for at least another month, maybe two, if she was lucky.

She'd decided she had the right to use him to prove her abilities. In that amount of time, she could ably demonstrate her talents. Then, when she asked to be relieved of that job, everyone would know it wasn't because she couldn't do the work.

Then she'd announce her pregnancy, when someone else was his accountant. Since the transfer would have already been made, it wouldn't occur to Jack to ask about her. He'd probably be too angry.

So she had her strategy all laid out. What could go wrong?

Checking her watch, she realized she could be late for the initial step, breakfast with Jack. She ran back to her desk to grab her purse and walk the three blocks to the diner.

Why had Sharon asked him to breakfast?

Last week, she hadn't even wanted to share a cup of coffee with him. She was up to something, but he didn't know what. He was going to hold in reserve his decision to have her taken off the job. He could spare some time to see what she was up to.

When he entered the diner, the morning rush was over and the noon rush hadn't begun. And Sharon hadn't arrived.

"Table for one, sir?" the waitress asked, picking up one of the plastic menus.

"No, I'm meeting someone." He looked back over his shoulder and caught a flash of red. "I believe this is her now."

Sharon came through the door, panting slightly. "Sorry I'm late," she said and drew a big gulp of air.

"Take it easy. I'm not worth all that running," he told her, secretly pleased that she thought so.

The waitress led them to the same booth they'd shared Friday night. As they slid in the waitress turned and grabbed two glasses of water from the station beside her.

"Here you go. Now, do you need time to read the menu, or are you ready to order?"

"Give us a minute, please," Jack said with a smile.

When they were alone, he asked, "Nothing's wrong, is it? I don't have another disaster on my hands, do I?"

"No, of course not. Everything's fine." She stopped to take a long drink of water. "I hate being late."

"Okay." He opened his menu, but he kept his gaze on her over the top. He already knew what he'd order.

He left her in peace until the waitress came back. Sharon ordered French toast and he asked for two eggs over easy, bacon, hash browns and wheat toast.

"Don't you worry about your cholesterol?" she asked.

He couldn't hold back a grin. "I don't think your breakfast is any healthier than mine, young lady, so don't go preaching health foods to me."

He was charmed when she blushed. "I don't usually eat out at breakfast, so I indulge myself."

She ran the tip of her tongue over her lips, and he wanted to indulge himself, too. At breakfast time. It wasn't often he got aroused so early in the morning, but then, he'd never had breakfast with Sharon.

"I like you in red. I wouldn't have thought it would look good with your hair, but I would've been wrong."

"Thank you."

When she said nothing else, he stepped up to bat.

"So, what's the purpose of our meeting? So you could have breakfast out and get Kane or me to pay for it?"

She pressed her lips together. "I'm paying the bill. But I needed to talk to you in private."

"Honey, we could get a lot more private than this. My condo's not far away."

"And there are probably several hotels nearby where you would willingly rent a room so we could be comfortable."

Was she offering to sleep with him? His heart leaped at the thought. Then he returned to reality. "Money wouldn't be a problem, but I'm not stupid enough to believe that's what you have in mind."

"Thank you. It's not. I need to convince you that as long as I work for you, we have to avoid—what happened Friday night."

"No problem. I'd already decided to can you." That was rude, but she looked so prim and proper, so in control, he couldn't resist rattling her cage just a little. Because he wasn't in control. Not when it came to her.

"What? No!"

"Here you go," the waitress announced as she slid two plates in front of them. "Syrup's on the table. Here's a pot of coffee, and I'll go get your orange juice." She hurried away.

Sharon drew a deep breath. "Jack—"

He held up his hand. The waitress reappeared with Sharon's juice. When she'd gone, he put his hand down to pick up his knife and fork. "Eat your breakfast before it gets cold."

"No, I must—"

"Eat, before you pass out. I'm not going to discuss anything until you've finished your breakfast."

Slowly she lifted her fork and pushed the French toast around. He picked up the syrup and offered it to her. With a sigh, she drizzled it across the toast.

He breathed more easily as she slowly tasted her breakfast. For a minute, he'd been afraid she'd jump up and run. He'd overdone his teasing.

When he'd finished his breakfast, she hadn't even eaten half of hers. "You're a slow eater, Sharon."

"I've had all I want," she hurriedly said, wiping her lips with the paper napkin. "Can we talk now?"

"I guess," he said and blew out his breath. "Look, it isn't going to work—"

"Yes, it will. Just give me a month, Jack. If you don't want to work with me after a month, I'll go to Kane myself and tell him it's not working."

"What's the point?"

"The point is my future with Kane Haley, Inc. I've worked hard at my job and in school for eight years. If you ask for me to be replaced, they'll take my promotion and my raise away from me. And I need the money."

"Kane wouldn't—"

"Why wouldn't he?" she whipped back. "If I can't do the job, why would he want to keep me?"

"I wasn't going to tell him you couldn't do the work."

"In a month, he'll know I can do the work. If you have problems with me then, it won't be my job performance."

Damn! She was boxing him in. He couldn't offer to take care of her financially. She'd go ballistic on him and never even see him again. He couldn't guarantee Kane's reaction, either. What she'd said was a possibility.

He'd never taken advantage of a situation at someone else's expense if he could help it. Here, he could help it. He just had to keep his libido in control. He just had to show patience. He just had to be miserable.

"*If* I wait, what are the conditions?"

She seemed startled. "Conditions? Why, we keep it strictly professional. No—no touching," she assured him, her beautiful eyes earnest.

"No deal, sister," he assured her in gangster tones.

"But—but we can't—word would get back to the office. And we'd both be in trouble."

"How many people from the company live in your neighborhood?"

She blinked her eyes several times. Finally, she said, "None."

"None of them live in my building, either. If we're discreet, I don't see a problem."

"What are you suggesting?" she demanded, horror in her voice.

"I'm not trying to blackmail you into sleeping with me. But we can see each other, talk, get to know each other for a month. I'm not opposed to keeping the physical stuff on hold for a while."

He was kicking himself at that statement. Man, he'd be miserable the entire time. Where was his head?

"No touching?" she asked, clearly not believing him.

"Well, I think I should get one kiss a week. Say, on Friday night. Only one."

"So we'd go out on Friday and talk. Then you'd get one kiss."

"I didn't mean we couldn't see each other other nights. Just keep the kiss for Friday night," he said, hoping she'd didn't think he sounded too stupid.

"No, I can't go out more than one night a week, especially not right now. And we'd avoid being seen?"

"What do you mean, especially right now?" he asked, distracted. "You said you weren't sick."

"I'm not, but I have an energy—uh, crisis right now. I'm taking vitamins to correct it, but I have to be careful."

He wanted to whisk her off to a doctor at once. One he knew who would tell him the truth. But she wouldn't go. Now he'd get an ulcer worrying about her.

"Okay?" she prodded, and he realized she was waiting for his agreement to her rules. Hell, why not? He couldn't risk getting her fired. And he couldn't live without seeing and touching her, even if it was only once a week.

"Okay. So this Friday is our first date?"

"Yes. But we have to be where we can't be seen."

"Great. You can come to my condo. I'll rent some movies, have dinner delivered in. We'll make it casual. You can relax."

· * · * · *

That sounded heavenly. A quiet, casual evening, nothing to do but show up. And she'd get to spend it with Jack.

Was she making a big mistake? She didn't know. But she couldn't risk losing her job. Not now. She needed the insurance and her salary. Besides, she wasn't sure she could leave Jack cold turkey. This way, she'd know more about him.

When her child asked about his or her daddy one day, she could talk about him. Not say, "I have no idea, dear. I was a four-hour-stand in an elevator."

Chapter Ten

Sharon congratulated herself on Friday.

After their breakfast on Monday, she'd scarcely seen Jack. Her week had been calm, efficient. In fact, she'd begun to wonder if he'd forgotten their arrangement. She'd brought a bag with her, containing casual clothes to change in to when she got to Jack's condo.

But if she didn't hear from him within the next hour, she wasn't going to go. She couldn't. He hadn't given her directions.

Almost as if she'd willed it, her phone rang. "Sharon Davies, Special Projects," she said.

"Here are the directions to my place," Jack said without any preliminary politeness.

"I thought maybe you'd changed your mind," she said. It gave him the option if he wanted it.

"No. But I thought you'd call for my address. You didn't."

"No, I—I thought you'd call." She drew a deep breath. "Look, Jack, this probably isn't a good idea. Why don't we—"

"You gave your word." He didn't leave any wiggle room.

"Yes, I did," she said softly. "Okay, I'll see you about six."

"Here are the directions." They were very detailed...and very simple. She'd have no excuse. A five-minute walk would put her in the lobby of his building.

After hanging up the phone, she couldn't help noticing an excitement in her. "No! Don't do this!"

Alice leaned forward. "Were you talking to me, dear? I didn't hear you."

"No, Alice, I was talking to myself. Sorry I bothered you."

"Not a problem, dear. Oh, hi, Andy."

Sharon whirled around to discover Andy had rolled his chair silently to her desk. "Hi, Andy. Did you need something?"

"No, not really. Except I'm a little tired. I think I'll go on home. Can you handle everything?"

Sharon and Alice both stared at him. He hadn't left early in the entire eight years Sharon had worked for him.

"Andy, are you feeling all right? Do you want to go see a doctor?" Sharon asked.

"Oh, my goodness, Andy, you must be sick," Alice agreed.

"I'm not sick!" he exclaimed, frowning. Another unusual occurrence. "I just have a headache."

Alice bustled out of her chair and came around Sharon's desk to put one hand against his cheek. "Oh! You're running a fever, Andy. You are definitely sick!"

"Dagnab it, woman! Get your hand off me."

"I'll go home with you, Andy, and get you some medicine and some dinner," Sharon immediately volunteered. Then she remembered her previous commitment. "Oh, I forgot!"

"I hope you already have plans," Andy said. "You're too young to be sitting around tending to an old man."

"But Andy, you have to take care of yourself."

"I am. I have a neighbor who's a nurse. She's promised to come in and check on me. Now go back to work, both of you. You owe me another hour's worth."

He tried to sound so crusty and cruel, but neither woman was fooled. Alice patted him on the shoulder. Sharon reached for his hand.

"Take care of yourself," Sharon said. "I'll call tomorrow to see how you're doing."

He just wagged his head in disgust and rolled toward the elevators.

Sharon and Alice did as he'd ordered, though not because they thought he'd been serious. He even encouraged his workers to slip out half an hour early on Fridays. He told them he might not have a life, but they certainly should.

As everyone began to pack up and head home, Sharon kept working. She wasn't going to leave until a few minutes to six. Time for her to get some quality work done.

Half an hour later, she decided quality might not be the right adjective. She couldn't keep her mind on work. All she could think about was Jack, and how the evening would end. And, if she'd admit it to herself, how much she'd missed him this week.

Could she hang in there for three more weeks? It was difficult. But then she reminded herself that after three weeks, she wouldn't see him at all. Not even once a week. She'd have to go cold turkey then.

Did they sell Jack-resistant patches? She didn't think so. So she'd better enjoy it while she could. Her hand drifted down to cover her stomach. There was beginning to be a slight bulge. She'd need to do some shopping soon if she was going to continue to hide her little secret.

For tonight, she'd left her jeans at home. They were already too tight in the waist. Instead, she'd picked some gray sweats that would hide everything.

Everyone was gone. She decided she'd change here. Gathering her bag, she slipped into the ladies' room. When she emerged, she looked like she was ready for basketball in the school gym. Was she being too obvious?

No. Well, maybe. She hadn't dressed to be romantic. She'd dressed for comfort. But she was finding that she couldn't bear to be in work clothes any longer than necessary. She only hoped Jack had rented a good movie. Otherwise she'd probably fall asleep in the middle of it.

* * *

Jack checked his watch. Two minutes. She'd said she hated to be late, and it was two minutes until six. He was eager to see her. He'd stayed away all week. Not to please her, but because he had two new accountants on the other accounts, plus the forensic accountants still working in Roger's office. And the police were hovering, still trying to get a lead on Roger. It seemed he'd left town the day Jack confronted him, already prepared to disappear.

Jack was pretty sure he'd contacted Darla, his wife. She had called Jack every morning, sure he knew where her husband was. Today she hadn't called. He'd finally called her, and she hadn't wanted to talk to him.

Though he'd felt mean, he called the policemen in charge and alerted them.

The doorbell rang. Jack sprang to the door, then drew a deep breath. He didn't want to appear too eager.

"Oh, Sharon, right on time. Come in,"

He noted her casual dress. Probably a good idea. He didn't need to be tempted right now.

Another elevator opened. "Looks like our dinner is here, too." He waved to the two men pushing a small cart in front of them. The restaurant on the first floor of his building had an excellent delivery service.

Sharon stood back for them to precede her. Then she looked at Jack, not moving. "You said to be casual."

He was dressed in slacks and a shirt. With a tie and jacket, he would be prepared to dine anywhere. But he didn't mind casual. "I wasn't sure how literally you'd take it, but I'm glad you did. I'm tired of dressing up. I'll change while they set up dinner.''

He reappeared quickly in sweatshirt and jeans, socks on his feet but no shoes. She was sitting quietly on the black leather sofa.

The two men were standing at attention beside the table. ''Will there be anything else, sir?'' one of them asked.

Jack handed them some folded bills and escorted them out the door. ''Well, everything's ready,'' he said as he came back in. ''Are you hungry?''

''It smells wonderful,'' she assured him. ''Everything is so—so elegant.''

''I like your room better.''

She frowned. ''What are you talking about?''

''Your bedroom.''

''But it's old and—and it's not—'' she waved her arms around her.

''I know. It's warm and welcoming. It's a wonder I don't have a constant cold in here. And it's hard to relax without something poking me.''

For the first time, she relaxed, grinning. ''Then why don't you fix it?''

''I don't know how. Besides, usually all I do is sleep here.''

''It's a pretty expensive bed,'' she pointed out.

He pulled out a chair for her at the glass-and-chrome table. ''I know. How'd your week go?''

''Fine. Routine, which is soothing. Except Andy left early this afternoon.''

''And that's worrisome?'' he asked, noting the frown on her face.

"He's never done that in the eight years I've worked for him. And Alice said he was running a fever."

They discussed Andy's possible malaise in detail. Then Sharon asked about the new accountants he'd been working with. She knew them well, and Jack's comments were complimentary.

Then they talked about the movies he'd rented and he told an amusing story about the video store that he knew would delight her. By that time, they were at the dessert stage.

"Dessert? Oh, no, I couldn't. I've gained weight and I have to be careful."

"But I ordered it especially for you. It's strawberry shortcake."

"How did you know?" Sharon asked with a gasp.

"I called your mother the other night. We planned the meal between us."

Instead of appearing pleased, she was embarrassed. "You went to a lot of trouble, Jack. You shouldn't have done that."

"Why not? It was just a matter of a few phone calls, Sharon. I didn't slave over a hot stove."

She smiled, but it turned into a giggle.

"What?" he demanded, his eyebrows up.

"I just pictured you in an apron."

He grinned in return. It had been the most delightful meal. He didn't want it to end. Taking the two dessert plates, he put them on the table, then removed their dinner plates.

"I'm sure I don't have as much style as our two waiters, but it's more fun without them."

"Yes, it is. I thought—I thought the evening would be a real strain, Jack. I misjudged you. Next time we can meet at my house and I'll cook."

"Can you?"

She pretended indignation. Then she said, "We won't starve, but it won't be fancy like this."

"You've got a deal. And you can invite your mother and her friend to join us. I enjoyed talking to her. I'd like to get to know her better."

"Uh, we'll see," she said and plopped a big strawberry covered in whipped cream into her mouth, making it impossible to say more.

They returned to their easy conversation while they ate the dessert, and Sharon scarcely seemed to notice when they moved to the black leather sofa in front of his big-screen television.

He put in the movie *Overboard,* a comedy about a wealthy woman getting amnesia and thinking she was married to a poor slob with four boys. It had them both laughing. Every few minutes, Jack found a way to move a little closer. First he simply shifted over several inches. Then he offered her something to drink. He set the glasses, hers filled with milk, of all things, in front of them and sat down closer to her.

He was going to offer popcorn next as an excuse, but she gave him a better one. She shivered.

"You're chilly? It's all this glass. Let me get us a cover," he said. When he returned with the cover from his bed, he sat down next to her. "I'm going to share, if you don't mind. I'm cold, too."

Then he casually put his arm up behind her, a move he'd practiced long ago when he took girls to the local movie. It still worked. Soon she was practically in his arms. When she laughed, he felt it. When the movie grew serious, as, unfortunately, it seldom did, she burrowed against him, as she had in the elevator.

When the credits rolled, he realized she hadn't moved at all in a few minutes, and he carefully leaned forward to check on her.

She was sound asleep, and it wasn't even nine o'clock.

He definitely thought she should go to a doctor, especially when he had to shake her to wake her up.

He waited for his kiss until they were parked in front of her house. It had been too big a risk with a bed a few feet away. He couldn't trust himself.

But it was a most satisfying kiss.

Saturday morning, he lay in his big bed, against the many pillows and thought about Sharon lying beside him, sharing a lazy Saturday morning. He couldn't imagine a more perfect start to the day.

The grin was still on his face when he suddenly questioned what he was thinking. Sharon wasn't going to share his bed on a casual basis, whether she worked for him or not. He had no doubt about that truth.

Which meant he had to face the question of marriage.

Much to his surprise, what filled him was quite similar to the emotion when he pictured Sharon lying beside him. Where was his fear, his distaste at being linked to one woman?

It wasn't there. Because he was talking about

Sharon, a beautiful young woman inside as well as outside. She was a hard worker, someone who reached out to others, someone who believed in the best of everyone.

Would she betray him?

No, no more than she would betray her brothers and sisters. She'd sacrificed and worked hard to provide them with an education.

He put his hands behind his head and smiled. Marriage to Sharon would be wonderful. He couldn't wait.

Sharon was less sure on Monday morning than she had been the previous Monday that her plan would work. Friday night had been wonderful. Then Jack had called Saturday morning.

Her heartbeat had skyrocketed when she heard his voice. He'd wanted to see her that day, to spend more time together. Oh how she'd wanted to agree. But she couldn't. It was already too hard to leave him, to step back, to remember that they would not have a future.

And yet, here she was, excited that she might see him today. She purposely went to the job site on her way in to the office. She wasn't going to deviate from her schedule because of her need to see Jack. That would be weak.

Just as she was finishing with Pete, her cell phone rang. She seldom used it unless there was an emergency, so she felt worried as she dug it out of her bag.

"Excuse me, Pete," she said to the foreman. "I'll

only be a minute." She stepped away and answered the phone.

"Sharon?"

"Yes, Mom. What's wrong?" She had no question that there was something wrong. Her mother would never interrupt her work for something trivial.

"It's Evie. She eloped last night."

Evie was Sharon's baby sister, the last of the siblings in college. She'd begun her junior year this fall. "She did? Why—that's—who did she marry?"

"That no-good Harry Irving. Remember? You met him here at the house."

"Oh, yeah." And he was no-good. He didn't treat Evie well, and Sharon suspected Evie shared what money she had with him. "I'm sorry, Mom."

"It's worse than that."

"What?"

"She's dropped out of school and doesn't plan to go back."

Sharon froze. Her dream of providing all her siblings with a college education, no matter what the cost, had almost been achieved. Almost. She rapidly blinked her eyes, trying to turn away the moisture filling them.

She was being ridiculous. Evie had chosen her future. Sharon didn't have the right to choose for her. She told her mother goodbye and put her phone away.

But instead of returning to Pete and carrying on with her job, for a moment, she covered her face, trying to gather her composure.

Hands grasped her shoulders and turned her around, pulling her against a broad chest. She didn't have to ask who had come. She knew. The strong arms held her, a broad, muscled chest offered a resting place. Her security blanket. Jack Waterton.

"What's wrong, sweetheart?" Jack whispered as he held her close, his heart thumping. Pete had pointed her out to Jack as soon as he'd arrived, and he'd seen nothing else.

When she'd covered her face with her hands, he'd known something was wrong. Nothing could've kept him from her side.

"It's nothing," she said, raising her head, trying to smile.

"Tell me anyway."

"My sister Evie has eloped and dropped out of school. I'd dreamed of—of all of them finishing school but—"

"You gave her the opportunity, you and your mother, with herculean effort. It's not your fault."

"I know, but—" Much to his surprise and pleasure, she laid her face against his chest again, and he rested his chin on her head.

Then she stepped out of his embrace, her cheeks red. "I'm sorry. I—I shouldn't have embarrassed you like that. You must be getting tired of me asking to be rescued." Her laugh was brief and awkward.

He wanted to pull her into his arms and kiss her until she never wanted to leave.

"I—I must go. I haven't been to the office yet."

Before he could say anything, she pulled away from him and hurried away.

"Is she all right?" Pete asked.

''Yeah, she'll be all right. She just received disappointing news.''

''About work?''

''No, it was personal.''

''I guess you two have gotten very close,'' Pete said, avoiding looking at Jack.

Jack didn't answer at once. He was realizing his agreement with Sharon wasn't going to work. He couldn't hold back any longer. ''We're going to be married,'' he said firmly, staring in the direction Sharon had gone.

Chapter Eleven

Well, she'd just proven that she couldn't handle the situation. She had to go to Kane and tell him she couldn't do the job. All her plans were blown away.

Even worse, her heart was losing the battle. She couldn't put it at such risk. Jack was so overwhelmingly charming and warm and—and she could go on forever. But it wasn't appropriate for a business associate.

When she entered the office, her first question for Alice was about Andy. "Is he here? How's he feeling?"

"You know him. He says he's fine and we're a bunch of worriers." Alice rolled her eyes.

With a heavy heart, Sharon walked to Andy's door. "I hear you're all recovered. Is that true?"

"Of course. I rested all weekend and took medicine just in case I was sick, which, of course, I wasn't." Andy's relaxed smile was back in place. Not for long.

"I'm glad, because there's a little problem on the Waterton account, and I—I need to talk to you and Kane."

"What kind of problem? What is it?"

"I'd like to tell you both at once. I'll go call for an appointment."

When she'd told Maggie they had a problem with the Waterton account, she, after consulting with Kane, told them to come up at once. Sharon was glad. She wanted this pretense to be over.

When they reached Kane's office, Maggie showed them in at once. Kane stood, a smile on his face. "Come in. I'm glad we could touch base before Jack gets here."

Sharon thought she would pass out. "H-he's already called?"

"Just a couple of minutes ago. I stalled him for half an hour. I hope that's long enough."

"Yes, probably," she agreed with a sigh.

"So, Andy, do you want to start? I hope it's nothing serious."

"I don't know what's wrong. It's Sharon who wanted to tell both of us at once."

"Sharon?" Kane asked, his eyebrows raised.

"I don't think I should continue working on Mr. Waterton's project." She clenched her hands in her lap and waited for the reaction.

Andy gaped at her, unable to speak.

Kane also demonstrated surprise, but he quickly recovered. "And your reasons?"

"I—I have several. In the elevator, when we were trapped, we grew close. It's been difficult to maintain any distance between us. And lately…it's best that we don't work together.

"It wouldn't be the first time friends have worked together. With Andy's supervision, I don't think that would be much of a problem. How does Jack feel?"

Sharon stared at the man. He wasn't upset.

"I don't think—Jack may feel—I don't know." She thought frantically. There was only one other thing she could tell them that would allow her to leave gracefully. They would have to know soon anyway.

"There's one other thing. The other day, you asked if anyone in our department was pregnant. Well, I am. It's sapped my energy and made it hard to maintain my work schedule. I wouldn't want to shortchange Mr. Waterton in any way when we have so many competent employees."

"Sharon, are you all right?" Andy asked, frowning. "I didn't know you were involved with anyone. Are you marrying him?"

"No, I'm not, Andy. If you feel it necessary to take back the promotion you gave me, I'll certainly understand."

"No, of course not. You're too valuable to our department."

Sharon breathed a sigh of relief until she looked at Kane Haley. He was staring at her, his face white.

"Kane? Mr. Haley?"

"You're not marrying the father? Why not?"

Sharon stared back, surprised by his question. "I beg your pardon?"

"Uh, I know it's personal, but—but do you know who the father is?"

"Yes, I do." She took a deep breath, hoping to remain calm.

"Did you use a sperm bank?"

Why was Kane suddenly asking such weird questions? "No, I didn't. But if you still need someone to sit on the committee for the child-care site, I'll be glad to since we all now know I have personal interest in it."

"That's not important. When—how long—when will your baby be born?"

"In about seven months."

He jumped up from behind his desk and began pacing the room.

Sharon looked at Andy, wondering what was going on. He returned her look, as puzzled as she.

Finally, Andy said, "Kane? Are you all right?"

"Yes, but I need to talk to Sharon alone," he said, whirling around to face them.

"Okay," Andy agreed, "if that's all right with Sharon. And do you have any problem with her retaining her promotion?"

"No, none. It's okay, isn't it, Sharon?" He actually seemed anxious for her agreement.

"Yes, of course, Kane." If he was okay with her keeping her promotion, what did he want to talk to her about?

"All right then," Andy said. "I'll see you in a few minutes." Then he rolled out of the office, pulling the door behind him.

Kane began pacing again.

"Kane, what's wrong?"

"I need to ask you again if you visited a sperm bank. And I need you to be honest with me."

She didn't understand what was going on, but she had no problem being honest. "No, I'm quite sure I did not visit a sperm bank. I have never visited a sperm bank. This pregnancy was not planned, but I'm very happy about the baby."

"Then why aren't you telling the father?"

She licked her lips. "Because—because nothing can come from it. I'll take care of my baby."

"You're sure?"

"I'm sure."

He went back to his desk and sat down. "Uh, who do you think should replace you on the project? And I assume you'll be able to give advice to whoever it is."

"Yes, of course. I think the best person for the job is Will Janklow. He's not flashy, but he's steady and trustworthy and deserving of the break."

"Okay," Kane agreed.

Sharon began to wonder if he'd even heard her. He still seemed to be acting weirdly. He drummed his fingers on the desk. "You'll tell Andy we're agreed?" She nodded and he added, "Good. Okay, good."

"Will you tell Jack? Mr. Waterton?" she finally asked after a minute of silence.

"Oh, yeah, as soon as he gets here."

"Good. Thank you, Kane. I apologize again for having to back out of the job."

"No problem. Take care of—take care of yourself and the baby."

"Yes, of course." She got up and left his office before he began asking her about her layette for the baby. What a strange interview.

Jack stayed at the site, trying to concentrate on work details, but he knew he was just marking time until Kane could see him. He'd decided to go to Kane first. Then when he explained it to Sharon, he could assure her Kane wasn't going to fire her. Or he could offer her an alternative.

When Jack greeted Maggie, Kane's door opened, and he came out to shake Jack's hand and invite him into the office, but he wasn't smiling.

"Everything all right?" Jack asked as he sat down.

"Yeah, sure," Kane said, returning to the chair behind his desk. "Well, maybe. Hell, I don't know."

Jack was taken aback by Kane's state of confusion. "Can I help with anything?"

"No, it's personal. The new guys are working out, aren't they? I was sorry to hear your suspicions were correct."

"Yeah. Roger's probably skipped to Canada. He's disappeared. The police can't find him."

"So you won't get any recompense?"

"No, but that doesn't matter. I had to explain to his wife. She didn't appear to be aware of any wrong-doing."

"That must've been an awkward conversation."

"Yeah." Jack got the impression Kane's mind was elsewhere, probably on that personal problem he'd mentioned. "Shall I go to Andy's office and check with him, since he supervises the new guys?" He had no intention of going until he talked to Kane about Sharon, but first he wanted to make sure they were clear on the rest of the business.

"We could do it that way. But, first, I need to talk to you about Sharon."

Jack did a double take. Those were his words. "Uh, yeah, me, too. She's very good at her job."

"Yes, she is."

"But I'd like her to be taken off my project."

Kane started to speak, then stopped. "What? You don't want her working on your job?"

"No."

"But why? You said she was good."

This explanation was what Jack had dreaded. He didn't like mixing personal and business, but it had to be done to clear the way for the future he had planned. "You know that we were in the elevator together. Well, our—friendship has progressed beyond what is professional."

Kane stared at him, one eyebrow rising. "Oh?"

"Yeah, and I'm not willing to give that up. I have plans. So I think it would be best if we don't work together. Surely you have someone else who can do the job?"

"Of course we do. In fact, we've already selected him."

Jack frowned. "Wait a minute. You were already replacing Sharon? Why? You didn't fire her, did you?" If they had, they'd regret it, he promised himself.

"No, of course not. But she came in this morning and requested it."

Jack couldn't quite believe Sharon shared his vision of the future. "Why?"

"I think you should know the reason if you have plans for the future. I think her reason might affect them," Kane said, frowning. Then he leaped to his feet and began pacing.

"Kane?" Jack said, anxious to know what was going on.

"Well, I really shouldn't tell you, but she didn't say not to. And everyone will have to know soon. I'm not sure exactly how soon." His voice almost trailed off and he ended up by the window, staring out at the city.

"Kane?" Jack said again. "What are you talking about?"

"Sharon's reason for removing herself from that particular job. She's still going to work. I guess she thinks she'll need to, but I'd be willing— Damn it, she said it wasn't— But she's the only one with the right time frame—"

"Kane, we're friends and I have a lot of respect for you, but I'm going to slug you if you don't explain what's going on." He stood, keeping his eye on Kane.

"I didn't explain?" Kane asked in surprise. "I thought I—"

"No. You said she asked to be taken off my job, but you haven't given me a reason."

"She's pregnant, and I think it's my baby," Kane said without delay.

Jack stared at him. Finally, with pain, he asked, "You had an affair with Sharon?"

"No!" Kane ripped. "I wouldn't do that. She's

one of my employees. That would be—reprehensible."

"Then how could you think you're the father?" Jack demanded, still confused.

"It's a long story, but I gave sperm to a sperm bank for a friend. When I called to have it destroyed, they told me they'd made a mistake and given my sperm to someone who worked here."

"Did you ask her?"

"Yes. She told me absolutely no sperm bank was involved. Twice she told me. But it all fits." Kane began pacing again.

Pregnant? Jack stared into space, disturbed by this information, but he had no intention of abandoning his plans. Sharon was too important.

She'd told him there was no man in the picture when they were in the elevator. Otherwise, he might not have—his thoughts froze. He stared at Kane. "How pregnant is she?" he demanded.

"She told me she was about two months pregnant. You see, the time—"

Jack stepped toward Kane, his hands clenched. "That's not your baby!" he roared. "It's mine!"

"What? *You're* having an affair with Sharon?" Kane asked, stepping toward him.

"No! I'm not. I intend to marry her." He liked saying that. The more he said it the more he believed it to be true. Then he remembered the baby.

"But how can it be your baby any more than it is mine if you and she haven't—you know, been together."

Jack felt his cheeks redden. "It was in the elevator."

It took Kane a few seconds to comprehend his remark. "You mean you—you're kidding."

Jack straightened his shoulders. "No, I'm not."

"And you've been dating since?"

Jack shook his head again. "No. I didn't see her again until we met in your office. I didn't even know her last name. It doesn't matter. We're marrying."

"Good. You should give your baby your name," Kane said with righteous indignation.

"You're sure she's pregnant? You've seen proof?"

Kane stared at him. "You think I would ask one of my employees to show me proof of her pregnancy, rather than take her word? What's the matter with you?"

"I've been lied to before." He and Kane had become friends, but not close enough for him to reveal all his secrets. "I married my first wife because she told me she was pregnant. She wasn't." He suddenly sat down, his legs weak as he took in the fact that Sharon was pregnant. Then he caught himself. He believed her? Without proof?

He did.

So when was she going to tell him?

"Did she say what she was planning to do?" he asked.

Kane sat down behind his desk. "When I asked her who the daddy was, she said she wouldn't say. I asked her if she was going to tell him, and she said no, it wouldn't change anything. There was no future there."

Cold shivered through him. She didn't plan to tell him. So what was she going to do? Disappear?

Something else occurred to him. "That's why she keeps falling asleep, why she wouldn't drink wine the other night."

"Yeah, I hadn't thought of that."

There was a lot Jack hadn't thought about. But he wasn't disappointed. In fact, he was enchanted. He'd wanted his own family, not like his parents' kind of family. So he'd accepted his first wife's trickery and tried to create a family. He'd waited with incredible anticipation for the birth of his child.

Then nothing.

Now he could plan again. He could dream of the future, of his child. But it would be with a woman he loved, with a woman he could trust. With Sharon.

He jumped to his feet. "I've got to find her."

"Wait a minute. What do you plan to do?"

"I told you. I'm going to marry her!"

"You won't be able to do that today."

"No, but we'll get things straightened out today. We'll clear up all the misunderstandings." He left the office, not willing to discuss his plans with Kane. He wanted to talk to Sharon.

Sharon was in mourning.

Now that she'd quit working on Jack's job, she wouldn't see him anymore. Except probably to explain why she'd broken their agreement. She felt badly about breaking her word.

Not badly enough to keep to the bargain, however.

Her body couldn't handle the tension. Her heart couldn't handle the pain.

She'd called her mother to talk again about Evie's decision. Her mother said, as Jack had, that Evie had to make her own choices. They might not agree with it, but it was her choice. And if Harry didn't remain faithful, then Evie would learn a lesson of life.

"How are you feeling, dear? Are you upset? You need to remain calm for the baby," Edith said.

"I know," Sharon agreed with a sigh. "I hope this kid appreciates all the work it takes to be a mom."

Edith chuckled. "She probably won't until she goes through her own pregnancy."

For the first time, Sharon thought about her mother and her pregnancies, not as her mother, but as a young woman going through the same experiences. "You're right, Mom. Did I ever thank you?"

"In a million ways, dear. You're a wonderful daughter."

Another accountant came to her desk and she quickly ended the conversation and answered the pressing question he had. Then she tried to concentrate on her work.

Almost impossible.

She heard heavy footsteps hurrying down the hall and looked up. Why was whoever it was running? Nobody ever ran at Kane Haley, Inc.

But Jack Waterton didn't follow the rules. That much she did know. He came to a stop in front of her desk.

"We have to talk." His voice was rough, emotional, and she stared at him.

"I know I broke our agreement, Jack, but after this morning, I felt you shouldn't have to deal with my difficulties in your business. It's better this way."

She'd practiced those words in her head. It was different saying them aloud, with Jack staring at her.

"I agree."

That brief response shocked her. She shoved her chair back a little. Something was up. "Oh, good. Then we have nothing to talk about. I'll make sure the transition is smooth and—"

He slapped his hand down on her desk. "When were you going to tell me?"

"Kane said he would let you know." She was beginning to tremble inside, knowing something was wrong.

"I think it should've come from you."

"Jack, I had to clear things through Kane first. It's his company."

"This has nothing to do with him and you know it," he growled, frustration in his voice.

Out of the corner of her eye, she saw Andy silently roll out of his office. Good, she could use the support.

"Jack? Everything all right?" Andy asked, as if he and Jack were passing in the hall.

"Stay out of this, Andy. It has nothing to do with you."

Sharon gasped. No one spoke to Andy like that. Not in the face of his constant good cheer.

"Well, now, Jack, you're in my department, talking to one of my employees. I think most would agree that circumstance would be my concern."

"Tell him, Sharon," Jack ordered. "Tell him it's not his business."

"You're getting a good man in my place, Jack. You have nothing to complain about," Sharon said, her voice stiff.

"Damn it! I don't care about accounting. I care about you and the baby. Tell Andy we're talking about my baby. Tell him you're having my baby."

Sharon figured she didn't need to send out announcements. Jack had just taken care of notifying most of the building.

Taking a deep breath, she stood, then bent to pick up her purse.

"No, Jack, I can't tell him that. Because I'm not having your baby." Then she walked out of the office, leaving a stunned Jack staring after her.

Chapter Twelve

Sharon lay on her bed, the covers drawn around her. She'd managed to get home before she lost her breakfast. That event had left her shaky. She'd taken the phone off the hook, changed into sweats, and crawled under the covers.

The shaking had finally stopped, but she couldn't rest. She'd lied to Jack. At the time, she'd told herself her baby was hers and no one else's. She felt that way. She wasn't going to involve Jack in her life or her child's.

What was the point? If he married her because she was pregnant, he would leave. Marriage for the sake of the child sounded good in theory, but in reality there was nothing to hold two people together.

She wasn't going to have that kind of marriage.

But she'd have to tell Jack she'd lied to him. Now that he knew about the baby, she'd have to be honest.

And she wasn't looking forward to that conversation. He would undeniably be angry.

A sudden pounding on her front door left her shaking again. Jack. She didn't have to ask who was there.

Maybe if she stayed still, he would eventually go away. After several minutes of the pounding, she gave up on that theory. She crawled out of bed and made it to the door, holding on to the wall as she went.

"Jack?" she called, hoping to end the thuds falling on the door.

"Sharon? Open this door. We have to talk!"

"Jack, I'm sorry. I—I lied. But I can't—I can't manage any more today."

Silence. Then his voice came again, not yelling this time. "Sharon? Are you all right? Did you get sick?"

"Yes."

"Have you called the doctor?"

"Jack, it's because I'm pregnant. But I don't feel well, and I'm worried—it's not good for the baby."

"Let me in."

She rubbed her forehead. What could she do? She didn't have the strength to fight him. Wearily, she unlocked the door and stepped back.

Jack stood on the porch, staring at her. "You look terrible."

She put a hand over her mouth, pain filling her. She wasn't even attractive to him anymore. Tears in her eyes, she turned away, half lurching toward her bedroom.

"Is your mom at work?" he asked.

She ignored his question and continued down the hall to her bed.

Before she could reach it, he'd passed her and entered the room. "What are you doing?" she asked faintly.

"Packing you a bag. You're going to the hospital."

"No! I'll be okay. I just need to rest." She sank down on the bed, her head swirling. Jack ignored her, opening and closing drawers. He'd already found an overnight bag in the bottom of her closet.

"Jack, I'm not going to the—"

"Where are your nightgowns?"

"In the second drawer, but—"

He took out a nightgown and put it in the case, then closed it. Picking it up in one hand, he reached for Sharon with the other. "Come on, sweetheart."

"I just want to rest, Jack. I'll be fine."

"Yes, you will, because I'm going to make sure of it. We'll go by the emergency room and see what they think. Then I'll take you home."

"But I'm already—Jack, please, just let me rest."

By that time, he had her at the front door. He opened it and told her to wait there. Then he hurried across the grass to his car and put the case in the back seat. After opening the passenger door, he came back and swung her into his arms. She grabbed his neck, her head spinning again.

He tucked her into the car, circled it and slid behind the wheel, and they were off.

"The nearest hospital is—"

"Who's your doctor?"

She gave him the doctor's name. As he drove, he used his cell phone.

"No, I don't want to have Dr. Norman call me.

I'm in the car, driving my—Sharon Davies to the hospital. She's been throwing up and is pale and shaky. I think she needs to be checked. Please tell the doctor we'll be at the emergency room in about ten minutes. Tell her to meet us there.''

Sharon's eyes widened. She wouldn't have dared speak to her doctor—or a nurse—in such tones. ''Pregnant women throw up all the time,'' Sharon whispered. ''It's no big deal.''

''It's not just that. You've had a lot of tension. That can't be good for the baby,'' he pointed out.

Sharon's hand cupped her stomach. ''I—I tried to stay calm,'' she whispered.

''I'm not blaming you, sweetheart. If anyone's to blame, it's me, but it didn't occur to me that—that what happened in the elevator could—that seemed such a different time, almost as if it never happened. It was magical. There were times when I wondered if I imagined it.''

She closed her eyes and leaned back against the seat. She didn't want to talk about those hours spent in each other's arms. It had seemed a simple matter of life or death then. Things were a lot more complicated now.

''Kane thought it was his baby,'' he said.

Her eyes popped open and she stared at him. ''What? But we haven't—''

''I know. But it shook me up. He thought you went to a sperm bank.''

''He kept asking me about sperm banks, but I told him I didn't.''

"I think it was the fact that you didn't want to name the father, didn't plan on marrying him."

Sharon said nothing.

"Why didn't you tell me? You know I'll take care of you and the baby," he said, hurt in his voice.

"I don't want any duty daddy, there because he has to be. It wouldn't last long, and both the baby and I would be hurt. I'm making good money now. We'll manage."

He pulled into the emergency room parking lot and parked. She didn't think the trip was necessary, but she'd accepted that she was going to be examined to satisfy Jack's concerns, so she got out of the car. Before she could even take a step, he appeared beside her and scooped her up into his arms again.

"Jack, I can walk," she protested, even as she put her arms around his neck.

He just kept walking.

From inside, someone saw them coming. Sharon supposed eleven in the morning wasn't the busiest time for emergency rooms, because a male nurse came out the door pushing an empty wheelchair.

"Good morning, sir. Put her right in here," he said, gesturing to the wheelchair.

Jack did so, and Sharon immediately felt bereft without his closeness. She scolded herself.

They reached the nurses' desk.

"Your name?" a nurse asked her.

"Sharon Davies."

"Where is your insurance card?"

Sharon looked at Jack. "Did you get my purse?"

He frowned at her. "No. I didn't think of it."

"I don't have it. Look, I don't really need to be—"

"I'll get the information," Jack snapped. "Where's a phone?"

With a sigh, the nurse shoved the phone on the counter toward him. "You can use this one while we take your wife in an examining room and get her settled. What's the problem, dear?"

"I'm about ten weeks pregnant and I've had a lot of stress. I vomited quite a bit and it left me shaky. He insisted I be checked," Sharon explained, avoiding Jack's gaze.

The nurse sent Jack a superior smile. "Men. They always panic over the smallest things. But since you're here, it won't hurt to check." And she wheeled Sharon away.

"Andy?" Jack said as soon as the man answered the phone. "I've got Sharon here at the hospital, and I need her insurance information."

"Is she all right?" Andy demanded at once.

"Sorry, I didn't mean to alarm you. She's been throwing up and looked like hell. I wanted her checked out."

"I'll be there in five minutes and I'll have all the information you'll need."

"Thanks, Andy."

He hung up the phone just as the nurse came back to the desk alone.

"Where is she?"

"Behind curtain number five. But don't upset her. We want her to stay calm."

"Right. A man in a wheelchair will be here in

about five minutes. He'll have all the information. When he's finished with that, tell him where to find us.''

"Now, Mr. Davies, we can't let just anyone into the emergency rooms. Unless he's family. Is he her father?''

"No, but he's the closest thing to a father she has. And he has a very calming affect on her. Let him in.''

"Well. I know how to do my job, Mr. Davies. You'd better go join your wife.''

Jack opened his mouth to say a few things, then shut it again before he had. If he told her who he was, she'd figure out he wasn't Mr. Davies and he'd be left out in the lobby.

"Five, you said?'' he asked as he was walking away.

"Yes.''

When he found the draperies marked five, he cleared his throat. "Uh, Sharon?''

"Yes?''

Her voice was faint and he opened the curtains at once to find her in a hospital gown, tucked into a hospital bed. Her sweats were folded on the only chair. He stepped to the bed and kissed her lips briefly. Then he pushed back her hair, traced her cheek and caught her chin between his fingers.

"You scared me.''

"I didn't mean to. Jack, we have to talk. I appreciate your concern—''

He stopped her with a kiss. "That dragon nurse said not to upset you, or she'll make me go away.

We're going to have plenty of time to talk. You need to rest right now.''

"Did you get the insurance information?'' she asked.

"Andy's getting it. He'll be right over.''

"Oh, he shouldn't have to—''

Another kiss. "Rest.''

The curtain parted and Dr. Norman stepped into the small area. "Hello, there, Sharon. How are you?''

"Oh, Dr. Norman, I'm sorry—''

The doctor shushed her, picking up her wrist and taking her pulse. Then she listened to her heartbeat. "Let's have you sit up and breathe deeply through your mouth,'' she instructed.

"I think everything's all right except you're over-excited and a little dehydrated. I'm going to set up an IV and I'd like to do an ultrasound, if you don't mind. I can't promise the insurance will completely cover the expense, but it will reassure us everything's fine.''

"Yes, please,'' Jack said at once, not consulting Sharon.

The doctor turned and looked at him. "And who might you be?''

"I'm Jack...the father of the baby.'' He was afraid to say his last name in case they threw him out.

"Ah, I see you decided to tell him. Good.''

"I didn't tell him. Someone else did,'' Sharon said, not looking at him. "That's why I—things got difficult.''

"Sir, I don't know what the two of you will work out about this child, but your job right now is not to upset Sharon.''

"I'm trying to take care of her, Doctor. And I'll do so in the future."

"No wife to interfere?"

Jack stared at her. "No, no wife…yet. Sharon will be my wife as soon as I can arrange it."

"Good for you," Dr. Norman said in approval.

Sharon looked from the doctor to Jack, both smiling, and closed her eyes.

Jack ended up in a corner of the curtained-off area. One nurse was putting in an IV. Another was rolling in a machine. Then she began preparing Sharon for the ultrasound. He wasn't sure what was involved, but if they were going to look at his child, he was, too.

The doctor had turned away to speak to another doctor. She stepped back inside the curtain as the nurse was spreading gel on Sharon's stomach. Jack watched in fascination and decided he could definitely see a rounded area that he didn't remember feeling when they'd made love.

"Jack," the doctor said, and he shifted his gaze. "If you want to see your baby, your best position will be on the other side of the bed at Sharon's head."

He took that position and also picked up her hand, taking it first to his lips, then holding it against his chest.

In a moment, he saw a vague picture with a strong heartbeat. He almost fell to his knees. His wife hadn't wanted him involved in her pregnancy. He'd never gone to the doctor with her.

"Sharon," he whispered, leaning down. "Honey, can you see? Do you see our baby?"

"Yes," she said, squeezing his hand. "I see."

"Good," the doctor said briskly. "Very strong heartbeat. I thought so." She stepped back from Sharon's bed, and the nurse began cleaning up, wiping the gel away. "You have nothing to worry about today, young lady, but I want you to take it easy for several days. Stay home from work. Then come to my office next week and I'll see if you can resume normal activities."

"Thank you, Doctor," Sharon said, not smiling. Jack put the hand he'd been holding back under the cover, kissed Sharon's cheek and followed the doctor outside the curtain.

"You're sure?"

"I don't lie, Jack. But I don't want her dealing with a lot of stress."

"No, I'll see to it," he assured her. Then, having spotted Andy, he called to him. "Over here."

The doctor excused herself, and Jack greeted Andy. "She's in here. Let me see if they've got her tucked back in." He peeked into the curtain area. "You ready for Andy?"

She nodded.

Jack pulled back the curtain so Andy could roll his chair in.

"Andy, you should've sent someone so you didn't have to come so far," Sharon said.

"It wasn't a problem. I took a taxi," Andy said with a grin. "Besides, I would've just worried about you if I hadn't come. What did the doctor say?"

"She's rehydrating me. Then I can go home, right, Jack?"

"Right, sweetheart," he agreed, not bothering to discuss what home he was taking her to.

"Good. When will you be back at work?"

"Doctor said she should take the rest of the week off," Jack said. He didn't want any misunderstanding on that point.

"Jack, I'm not sure that's necessary," Sharon protested. "I think I can—"

"You'll follow the doctor's orders," he said sharply, determined on that point.

She tried to sit up, her temper rising. The nurse who was tucking her in said, "Remember you're supposed to stay calm." She gave Jack a pointed look. Then she added, "In half an hour, we're going to bring you a luncheon tray. Until then, I suggest your visitors let you rest."

Jack had never been so summarily invited to leave. He glowered at the nurse, but Andy tugged on his sleeve. "Why don't you push me out to the lobby, Jack? I'm a little tired from my rush down here."

"Okay," Jack said, his voice gruff. He stepped to the bed and gave Sharon another of those gentle kisses. "I'll be back," he promised. Then he pushed Andy to the lobby.

"Are you all right, Andy?" Jack asked as he took one of the plastic chairs beside Andy's wheel chair.

"I'm fine. I just didn't want you getting in a fight with the nurse in front of Sharon."

"I wouldn't—well, maybe I would. I don't see why I had to leave."

"Because you and Sharon haven't worked everything out."

He hung his head. "I know. When I got there, she told me she'd lied, the baby is mine. But she looked so miserable, so sick, all I could think about was getting her some care. She needs to rest. She falls asleep every time I'm with her. Except today."

"Have you two spent much time together? I mean, you must've since it's your baby, but I didn't know—"

"It was in the elevator. I've already told Kane, and I'm telling you, but I know Sharon won't want that spread around."

Andy stared at him.

"She was having hysterics and I was trying to comfort her. One thing led to another. It's hard to explain."

"And in the future?"

"I'm marrying her. She and the baby will be with me."

"There's just one thing, Jack. She doesn't trust men. She said one time that there was no point in marrying a man, because he'd leave anyway. You're going to have a hard time convincing her."

He'd already suspected as much, but Andy's warning confirmed it. What could he do to convince Sharon that he would stay?

When Sharon's IV had finished, she slowly opened her eyes as the nurse removed the needle. "Does this mean I can go?" she said sleepily.

"Yes, it does, and your husband is here to take you," the nurse said, smiling.

Sharon looked up to find Jack behind the nurse.

She should tell them he wasn't her husband. But why bother? They wouldn't be back here together.

"Sir, if you want to take her in the hospital gown, instead of dressing her again, just wrap the blanket around her and put her in the chair. You can drop the gown and blanket off later." Then she added sternly. "If you don't, we'll add it to the bill."

"That would be easier, thank you," Jack agreed.

Sharon didn't protest. Jack picked her up and she snuggled against him. She shouldn't, she knew, but he was so comforting. Then he put her in the wheelchair.

"She should go right back to sleep when she gets in bed. Wake her for dinner, then back to bed. Okay?"

"Got it. Thanks."

It didn't sound too exciting, but Sharon kind of liked that schedule. Of course, her mother wouldn't be home from work for several hours, but she'd leave her a note.

The transference to the car was smooth, as was the ride. In fact, Sharon didn't remember the ride. The next thing she knew, Jack was lifting her again. It seemed darker than it should be, but maybe the sun was behind a cloud. What did it matter?

She next came awake as Jack withdrew his arms. "Jack, don't go!" she protested, her own voice waking her completely. "Oh, I didn't mean that. I— Thank you for taking care of me."

"My pleasure. And I'm not going."

He pulled the cover over her, then pulled the hospital blanket from beneath her. "There you go, sweetheart. Sleep tight."

With a sigh, she closed her eyes. The touch of his lips barely registered. She was asleep.

The next time she awoke, she was feeling remarkably better. So much so that she recognized Jack's voice at once. "Jack? You're still here."

He came into sight. "I am. Why would I leave?"

"Well, you might need to get home or something."

"I *am* home."

That stopped Sharon. She hadn't seen Jack's bedroom when she'd visited the Friday before. But it was obvious this wasn't her bedroom. "Why did you bring me here?"

"To take care of you. I've got dinner ready. Do you want it here in bed, or will you come to the table?"

"I'll come to the table. Then I'll go home. I'm sorry. I didn't intend for you to go to so much trouble. Oh," she exclaimed, looking at her wristwatch. "I need to call Mom. She'll be worried."

"I called her."

Sharon stopped getting out of the bed. "You did? Is she all right? What did she say?"

"She offered to come over at once, but I told her it wasn't necessary."

The thought of her mom was comforting, but Sharon chastised herself. She was an adult. She could get home by herself. "Of course not. I'll go ahead and leave now while it's still daylight."

"No, you'll eat first. *If* you leave, I'll take you. You don't need to be riding the El. It's too rough."

"I ride it all the time. What do you mean—why did you say *if*? Of course I'll be leaving."

He stepped to his closet and dragged out a dark robe. "You may want this so you won't get a draft."

She looked down her back to discover the gap between ties. "Oh! Thank you."

Before she could return to her argument, he seated her at the table and put a plate of food in front of her. Hunger made the decision for her. The hospital food hadn't been particularly filling and she was hungry.

They ate in silence, a real contrast to their last meal together. She watched him from beneath her lashes, wondering what he was thinking. He'd been wonderful today, taking care of her, even if he was autocratic. But they were going to have to discuss the future. She supposed she should promise to let him visit his child. But it would break her heart every time.

She put down her fork. "You can visit our baby."

He smiled. "Good for me."

"If you don't want to, it's all right."

"Eat your dinner."

When she'd finished, she said, "I'll go change so you can take me *home*."

"Before you do that," he said calmly, "I have something to discuss with you."

It had to come sometime. She drew a deep breath. "Okay."

"I want to marry you."

She opened her mouth to tell him it wasn't necessary, but he held up a hand. "It's my turn. You can talk in a minute."

She nodded.

"I want to marry you because I love you like I've never loved anyone. I want to wake up with you beside me. I want to share the trials of my day with you. I want to take care of you and my child. I want other children. I want to walk through life together."

Sharon stared at him. Finally, she said, "That's a beautiful speech. I'll always remember it. But we both know you're proposing because of the baby. You've already been trapped in a marriage once. I won't do that to you. As I said, you can visit the baby if you want, but it's not necessary. I'll take good care of her."

"Him. I'm pretty sure it's a boy."

"You are? It's too early to tell."

He smiled, a smile that made her want to trace his lips, to kiss that smile right off. "I can tell."

"You can not!"

"We'll see in seven months."

She blinked several times to disperse the tears. "Jack, it's all right. You don't have to pretend."

"I'm not pretending. Just a minute." He got up and crossed the room to the coffee table in front of the couch. He picked up a folded piece of paper and came back. "Here's our prenuptial agreement."

She stared at him, unable to control the tears that rolled down her cheeks.

He knelt beside her chair. "Don't cry, sweetheart. I have to explain. When you marry me, you have to know you're not getting a great family. We're majorly dysfunctional. We don't touch, we don't care, we aren't there for each other. The only thing I really care about is my company. I built it from scratch. By myself. I'm so proud of it."

She nodded, the tears still coming down.

He unfolded the paper. "But my company, my creation, means nothing to me compared to you and our baby. This paper says that if I leave you, if I betray you in any way, you get my company, lock, stock and barrel."

The tears were coming down faster and she shoved at the paper. "I don't want your company."

"That's the point, Sharon. I don't want it either if I can't have you and our baby. I'm not going to leave you. I may get angry with you. If I do, we'll have a big fight. But I'm not leaving, no matter what."

He stood and pulled her into his arms.

"Jack, are you sure?"

"Oh, yeah. I'm sure. Will you marry me?"

"Yes," she whispered just before her lips met his.

A week later, she was back at work, relaxed and happy, with a wedding planned for the weekend after this one. She couldn't believe how her life had changed.

"Morning, sweetheart," Jack said, as if she weren't living in his condo. As if they hadn't woken together this morning.

"Jack, what are you doing here?"

"I want you to come with me," he said, holding one hand behind his back.

"I should tell Andy if—"

"He knows. Come on."

"Where are we going? Do I need my purse?"

"Nope." He led her to the lobby on her floor and pushed the down button. An elevator stopped, but he wouldn't let her get in. "Not that one."

When the one on the end opened, *their* elevator, he tugged on her hand and led her into the elevator.

"What are you doing, Jack?"

He said nothing, watching the lights on the panel. Suddenly, he pushed the emergency button, stopping the elevator.

"Jack!"

"Easy, Sharon. I'll start it again in a minute." Then he pulled his hand out from behind his back, and held before her a long-stemmed red rose and a ring box.

"I think it's about time we replace those old memories with some new ones." He went down on one knee. "Sharon Davies, will you marry me, be my wife for the rest of my life, love me and never leave me?"

"Yes, I will, as long as you promise the same," she said softly.

"Done!" he exclaimed and stood up. He opened the ring box and a beautiful diamond ring sparkled. He took it out and put it on her finger. "Now it's official," he whispered and kissed her finger. "You're my elevator bride."

"Yes, and we're definitely going up. I love you, Jack!"

* * * * *

*Turn the page for a sneak preview
of the next*

HAVING THE BOSS'S BABY *title,*

A PREGNANT PROPOSAL

*Matt and Jen's story!
by rising star Elizabeth Harbison
on sale in November 2001 from
Silhouette Romance…*

And don't miss any of the books in the
HAVING THE BOSS'S BABY *series,
only from Silhouette Romance:*

*WHEN THE LIGHTS WENT OUT…,
October 2001
by Judy Christenberry*

*A PREGNANT PROPOSAL, November 2001
by Elizabeth Harbison*

*THE MAKEOVER TAKEOVER, December
2001
by Sandra Paul*

*LAST CHANCE FOR BABY, January 2002
by Julianna Morris*

*SHE'S HAVING MY BABY!, February 2002
by Raye Morgan*

Chapter One

When Matt got to Jen's office, she was on her way out. She had her coat and scarf on, and in one mittened hand she held a doughnut. As she tried to close her office door, her keys slipped out of her other hand.

Matt swooped in and bent down to pick them up for her. "Hey," he said, handing her the key chain.

Her face flushed prettily, making her green eyes sparkle even more than usual. "Hey," she said back. "Thanks. What are you doing down here?"

"I came to see you, actually. Can you spare a few minutes?" Honestly, he'd never seen such a beautiful example of the 'bloom of pregnancy'. Jen had it in spades.

"Now?"

"I need to have a talk with you."

Her face paled. "You're not firing me, are you? I know I'm going to need some time off, but…"

"No, Jen, no!" He was so touched by her unexpected show of vulnerability that he wanted to take her into his arms. "Actually, I was going to pick your brain about child care. Kane's interested in putting a center on-site for you and the other parents here."

Her shoulders relaxed. "That would be a godsend."

"Great. Maybe we can hammer out enough of the details to get something started."

"So whose idea was the day care? Yours?"

He shook his head. "I'd like to take credit, but it was Kane's idea."

She looked surprised. "No kidding?"

"No kidding."

"Wow. He's really been softening up lately. I saw him about ten minutes ago and he seemed unusually interested in how I'm feeling. I didn't even know he knew who I was."

"He knows who you are. You're hard to miss."

She made a face, gestured helplessly at her belly, then cocked her head ever so slightly, but before she could respond, a round, bespectacled man neither of them recognized called, "Miss Martin?" from down the hall in front of them.

Matt and Jen turned to see him trundling toward them, sweating and holding a folder of some sort.

"Yes?"

"Jennifer Martin?" the man asked, mopping his brow with his forearm.

A cannonball of apprehension lodged in Matt's stomach. Instinctively he stepped in front of Jen and started to ask who the man was, but before he could get a word out, she said, "Yes, I'm Jennifer Martin."

The man shoved the folder roughly into her hand and said, "These are for you." Then he waddled back down the hall without another word.

Jen frowned and tried to look at the folder but lost her grip and dropped it. "Would you mind picking that up, Matt?"

"Not at all." It went against his instincts to pick up someone else's private papers, but he couldn't very well stand there and make her bend over to get them. He lifted the folder and held it out to her.

She gestured that she was holding keys in one hand and her doughnut in the other. "Would you look?" she asked with a charming smile. "Who's it from?"

He looked at the return address. "Sedwick-Armour."

She rolled her eyes. "Ack. I should have known. It's Philip's father. I wonder what he wants now. An old pair of socks that Philip left at the apartment, no doubt. Open it up."

"Jen, I really don't think I should."

"Oh, come on."

With a shrug, he opened the envelope and pulled out the papers. Just glancing at the first page made his heart sink.

"Matt, jeez, what's the matter?"

Matt just looked at her. Jen was eight months pregnant and single. This was going to be devastating. And it was absolutely the last thing in the world she needed right now.

"What is it, Matt? What do they want?"

He gave her hand a squeeze and swallowed hard. "They want the baby, Jen."

CALL THE ONES YOU LOVE OVER THE HOLIDAYS!

Save $25 off future book purchases when you buy any four Harlequin® or Silhouette® books in October, November and December 2001,

PLUS

receive a phone card good for 15 minutes of long-distance calls to anyone you want in North America!

WHAT AN INCREDIBLE DEAL!

Just fill out this form and attach 4 proofs of purchase (cash register receipts) from October, November and December 2001 books, and Harlequin Books will send you a coupon booklet worth a total savings of $25 off future purchases of Harlequin® and Silhouette® books, AND a 15-minute phone card to call the ones you love, anywhere in North America.

Please send this form, along with your cash register receipts
as proofs of purchase, to:
In the USA: Harlequin Books, P.O. Box 9057, Buffalo, NY 14269-9057
In Canada: Harlequin Books, P.O. Box 622, Fort Erie, Ontario L2A 5X3
Cash register receipts must be dated no later than December 31, 2001.
Limit of 1 coupon booklet and phone card per household.
Please allow 4-6 weeks for delivery.

I accept your offer! Please send me my coupon booklet and a 15-minute phone card:

Name: _____

Address: _____ City: _____

State/Prov.: _____ Zip/Postal Code: _____

Account Number (if available): _____

---

097 KJB DAGL
PHQ4012

Next Month From Steeple Hill's

Love Inspired®

LOVE ONE ANOTHER

by *Valerie Hansen*

Romance blooms when Zac Frazier and his little boy move into Tina Braddock's quaint neighborhood. Although the compassionate day-care worker knows the pitfalls of letting anyone get too close, she can't resist extending a helping hand to the dashing single dad and his adorable son. But a heavy-hearted Tina fears that their blossoming relationship will wilt if her shameful secret is ever exposed. Turning to the good Lord for support, Tina can only pray for the inner strength she desperately needs to trust in the power of love....

Don't miss
LOVE ONE ANOTHER
On sale November 2001

Love Inspired®